ITERUM

Tales of Mystic Metamorphoses

YASHASWINI BALASUBRAMANYAM

INDIA • SINGAPORE • MALAYSIA

ISBN 979-8-88935-965-4

For my parents and my sister.
<3

Stories

1

A Puppet and His Master

TODAY
3:00 am

I have seen many deaths in all the time that I have lived. I have always handled them well.

For instance, when my parents were leaving me behind in this world, I had sat looking at them without flinching.

I may have been an emotional wreck after the moment of death, others', passed. But during the dying, I didn't so much as bat an eyelid. Never. That is how collected I was.

Or, maybe, I had been incapable of grasping the gravity of the situation at that moment.

I...am not sure if the usage of the word 'gravity' is all that appropriate here since I am discussing death, which happens when gravity fails severely. Tell me, how else are we able to go *all* the way to the stars without so much as a hiccup! That's it. Death happens, when gravity loses control over your soul.

These thoughts. This is what I am talking about. When I saw others die, I barely had thoughts, I am sure.

But now that *I* am dying, thoughts are all I have. I am feeling so many feelings, I can't point to one.

I am afraid. I feel lost. I am swimming in a pool of regrets even as my core departs at a snail's pace.

I feel relieved, for I do not have to wage battles all alone, anymore. I feel grief; I am positive I am allowed to grieve my own death. I want to laugh; because, life is hilarious.

But more than anything, I feel nostalgic.

I find myself going through my life in no particular order. Unintentionally. All I see are little films of moments from the past. Like ants in a row, they crawl in front of me, one after the other. I go back in time and relive them. I have nothing else to do, after all.

Surprisingly, the films are plastered with the face of the one man whose existence is what has driven me out of the world. *Driving* me out of the world.

Tej.

He is the reason I am having to quit being. But I would not have lasted all this long, if it weren't for him.

Now he lies still, unflinching, his eyes boring into me without any trace of remorse. Peppy too, seems to stare at me mockingly. The audacity!

I think of my times with Tej. I know I have done everything that I could, for him. Yet, my leaving does not affect him at all.

It is saddening.

The memory films are glitching. My time-traveling has come to an abrupt halt. The past and present have become one. I am stuck in the happenings of yesterday.

Yesterday is my *now?*

Yesterday is my now.

Nobody should have to live their own death twice.

But while I am at it, I will allow you a glimpse of the day, for I need someone to witness the bloodshed. Besides, who better to tell Tej's story than I? Life may well be his. But the narrator, it always will be me.

YESTERDAY

04:30 pm

Tej. Hmmm. He is the only association I have. Without him, I wouldn't exist. Nor would he, without me. I like to think so.

We have a bond so strong; it is inexplicable!

He is not in front of me at the moment. But I always know what he is up to. It's like that with us. In fact, I know the look he would be wearing on his face right now.

He is getting ready for yet another of his shows. The famed ventriloquist and his round-faced puppet. You know ventriloquists, don't you? The ones that can make lifeless dolls seem to talk. Tej is one. Well, sort of.

Tej's heart is beating fast, and he is muttering lines to himself. In his line of work, what he says is of utmost importance. He can't afford to forget them; and he's afraid he will do exactly that.

Inside the puppet's throat, his hand is dripping with sweat. His. Not the puppet's. He expertly wipes it on the furry insides, like he always has. Now, the puppet's insides are moist with sweat. His, again. His performance will soon commence. Blinking continuously, he clears his throat to get rid of prickly thorn-like nothings that threaten to steal his voice. He looks weary, but there is a sparkle in his eyes. Because, he loves this part: the part where he performs. He always has.

He was seven, when he got onto the stage in their school. It was not a very big school, nor was the stage a very big one. That's why he was the recipient of a deafening applause after his first performance. Everyone had witnessed his splendour, and he was not ignorant to it. A little boy with a hole in the sole of both of his shoes, he had walked on the stage delivering his lines, with his head held high. He went on to portray many more roles before the world tagged him an upcoming marvel.

But life is seldom that predictable. No time to get into the details, but he has come a long way from where he once was. A long way backwards. He is no theatre artist, nor a marvel. Today, even as he grasps onto Peppy the puppet's throat, he knows his reality. The reality where *he* too, like Peppy, is a puppet, and *I,* his master. Or, does he?

It's his eighth show for the day, and he can't wait to get home. They are in matching attires, Peppy the puppet, and Tej. Because, a few weeks ago, he spent most of his month's salary on clothes. Matching clothes for the puppet and the master. Adding a splash of colours to both their wardrobes will do wonders, he had told me.

Tucking his yellow shirt into his blue pants, he fans himself to drive away the panic. He hears the door click open. The audience is here. He urges himself to not break character, come what may. Sighing, and plastering a huge smile on his face, he bellows from within the kitchen as his puppet friend peeks out into the hallway.

"Well, who do we have here?", Tej asks in a cartoonish voice that every one of his previous audiences has loved.

"I am Peppy, your guide for the day", the voice seems to come from the puppet.

When he hears laughter and exclamation, Tej's sagging shoulders lift up. He peeks into the hallway from behind his round-faced puppet friend. He sees a woman, a man and two children; all dressed in red. They flash an eager smile as the ventriloquist walks to them, with his puppet buddy.

"Here to see the house, are you? Well, this house looks complete with you adorabubble children, and you loving parents! Hop on, let us have a tour of your future house!", the puppet says to the amused family, flailing its empty sleeves in the air.

With their eyebrows raised dramatically, Peppy and Tej look around the living room. Chattering urgently among themselves, the two make a quick circle around the family in red; thus, making the onlookers go a full circle themselves. The performers glide across the hall and settle on the couch. Peppy lets out an exaggerated gasp.

"Ah! To sit in your own home and one that's as beautiful as this, and to watch some TV!", the puppet sighs.

Then, it begins to fan itself. "Air conditioner, Tej?".

Tej pats the puppet on the head, while shaking his own. He reaches for the door to the balcony. Even as he pushes it open, the duo pretends to be lost in a daze.

"Ah, are we in the meadows? Where is this breeze coming from! What lovely breeze, Tej!", Peppy the puppet says. Pointing to the family, it goes on, "If this family in red is not getting this house, then let us do it! We ought to!".

The audience laugh at the two. Tej smiles within.

Tej is 29. He is a real estate sales guy who spends his day showing houses to people. It's a taunting job that he has subjected himself to, he often tells me. Selling houses that scream luxury, and then coming back to our cave with leaky roofs. Alright, there are no leaky roofs, nor is our home a cave. But the place is always dark. Lifeless. Stifling. I have no complaints, for it has worked in my favour. Tej, however, has yet to come to terms with his harsh reality.

"It's like waving a piece of fresh-cream cake in front of someone, when you know fully well that they are fasting and can't get a bite of it! That's how this job feels. I can never buy one of those houses…", he has sighed one too many times.

The apartment that he is attempting to sell is huge! He is going to be needing some time to finish this show. We will leave him to his performance, for I want to take you through his life. Our life.

We live in a cramped 'Studio apartment', as the estate guys put it. It has just enough light for the dwellers to guess if it's day or night outside. I have no one but him, and he has no one but me. If truth be told, there were many instances where he *could* have had more than just me in his life. The girl with a mole on her nose, to name one. She thought the world of him. He too had wanted her to move in with us. He should have known better than to make me feel left out. He did not. So, I took it upon myself to lay out his priorities in life in order. We had a small chat, Tej and I; and the girl with a mole on her nose never visited us again. But that's a story for another time.

We spend the most time together during nights. Every evening, he comes home to me whining about his life. And I offer him my advice. Advice that leaves no room for false hopes. Advice that keeps him grounded.

I am his go-to person, if I can say so. I had him promise me, long before he understood what promises meant, that it would always be him and I against the rest of the world. I have stuck to my end of the bargain, never wavering. But he is an unstable mess these days. So, there have been a few hiccups here and there, in our relationship too.

For instance, he used to be miserable about the bland profession that life had chosen for him.

A month ago, he woke up in the middle of the night, panting for breath. Sure, he did that every other night. But on that one, it was not *my* doing. I had not spoken to him as he slept, nor had I sung to him. He had woken up of his own accord, and blurted something shockingly stupid. He had said that he would begin to perform again.

"It does not matter if there is no stage to glorify me. I will make apartment-viewing a memorable experience for every family that steps into the house. That way, I can stay in touch with what I have always loved. I will get better at it, overcome my fears, and then chase my dreams.", he had said.

I was astounded. What was this overcoming and chasing that he was talking about? Never in our 13 years of association had I heard him say such things. He fell asleep with a silly smile plastered on his face. There wasn't a moment of doubt. No panic. Instead, it was I who was subjected to those novel feelings. I spent that night sitting by the foot of his bed, watching him sleep. I sang to him, and told him stories I had heard from my ancestors, about failure and its consequences at such an age. He had winced, but I got nothing more from him that night.

The next morning, he walked out the door with his left fist shoved into a round-faced puppet's throat. "Meet Peppy, the puppet!", he paused to introduce the silly thing to me before he left with a determined look on his face. A look that still sends shivers down my spine. Oh, how I hate puppets!

After hours of running up and down the floors of his workplace that day, he had finally gotten what he wanted: the permission to turn clients' apartment-viewing into performances.

That was the biggest disagreement we had had in all our years together. I was cowering when he came home that evening. He had decided to act on his own, not caring to know what I thought of his decision.

Would he forget all about me? Would he drive me away from this place I have been calling home?

I had waited in anticipation to hear what he had to say. He threw his shoes behind him, unbuttoned his shirt, and sat on the crooked chair by his study. He looked around our dark but spotless apartment and sighed.

"Am I doing the right thing?", he had asked.

I did not think he would address me after all his talks about dreams and chases. I was elated. Regaining my confidence, I went to lend him a shoulder to cry on.

He hit me with the possibilities of his life getting better. It was tough dragging him out of the pretty picture he had painted for himself in under a day. But I did it nonetheless. I made him believe otherwise. It was up to me to make him see the reality, after all.

That one night's blurting and the day's doing of his had cost me my peace; so much that I had to attend one of those support group sessions meant for our kind. The last I had been associated with them was before I met Tej; back in the days of my family's existence.

The venue was an empty ground beneath a tree that I would not have dared to visit alone. As the session went on, confessions were made, and questions addressed. I was a silent observer. I saw attendees of all age groups. Some, I was sure, were invisible to the naked eye. They looked like any moment could be their last. I was paralysed with fear. But there were also those that loomed over me. They were huge. Intimidating. I did not know we could grow to that extent. I wished then that I had had someone a lot less passionate than Tej!

As if reading my mind, the facilitator had said "As long as they hesitate, we will thrive, not just survive."

That made me hopeful.

Since that meeting a month ago, I have been prepared to tackle any more of Tej's tantrums if they ever came up.

But, while he has gone on putting up show after show for his clients, he has not pursued the matter any further. I do not hear him talk about chasing dreams. Not even in his dreams. He is no threat, I am convinced.

Perhaps I could outgrow every one of the attendees, some day.

STILL YESTERDAY
09:09 pm

Is it past 9 pm already? I can't help but feel uncomfortable. Because, it has been a few hours now, and I have had no access to Tej. It is new, and worrying. Never has an hour gone by where his fear did not eat him alive; so much that I could sense it all the way back in our damp little cave of an apartment. The last I heard from him today was a little while after he had bid goodbye to the family in red.

With them gone, he drank two jugs of water to soothe his throat, before sinking into the couch. Sitting still with his head in his hands, he had tried, and failed, to discover the meaning of life. His life.

When he was on his way back home, a pamphlet hit him out of nowhere; something about a play. He was flushed with fears. And then, I lost all access to him. I wonder what he is up to. When did he slip away?

I got carried away playing 'Narrator' perhaps.

STILL YESTERDAY
10:00 pm

The clock has struck 10. I hear keys, then a sigh. Tej is home. His attitude is different. He walks in with his shoes still on, and his sweaty shirt still buttoned. His eyes are distant. He looks red. But he is not angry. Nor is he worn out. His face has a look I have never seen before; that of exhilaration. Realization. Most of all, relief.

"So, I saw a play today…", he says out loud, smiling. If one were to see him talking thus, they would place him for an insane young man who talked to himself. They can't be blamed, for Tej was looking at the walls and furniture as he spoke. Only *I* knew that he was talking to me. Glad that he cared enough to address his day's adventures to me, I acknowledge him.

"I found a pamphlet that was an invite to a play. I was apprehensive at first. Because, the actors and the stage would only remind me of what I could not achieve. But something urged me to go, and go I did.", he says.

Had he met someone? Was he going to bring them home? Was he going to break his promise yet again? I don't have a good feeling about this. But there's nothing I can say now. Looking at him with growing resentment, I wait for him to talk. I am curious to know what it is that has given him the audacity to talk thus; without an ounce of fear in his entire being.

"When I went, there wasn't a soul in the auditorium. I considered leaving. But the stage…it came to life just as I turned to leave. There were lights. There was music. The show began…I was the only audience! 'Sit!', they said. I don't know why, but sit I did.", he smiles. I sigh.

"The play was about a group of aliens who are abducted. They are held captive in a dense forest where trees cover the very sky.

Chained to trees lest they attempt to flee, they are told to saw logs of wood. Then, to grate them into fine powder. None of the aliens asks why it is that they have to do so. Because, they are promised bread and wine, in exchange.

As time goes by, they carry on with their job like their life depends on it. No longer do they need to be chained, for they have long lost the will to escape.

Sometimes, they hear distant roars, or see a spark of blinding light through chinks between the rustling leaves.

"What lies there?", they wonder. Whenever they do so, a fire lights up within them. A fire of passion. But the burning dies the moment they realize that those distant lands can never promise them the wine and bread they have become accustomed to.

So, whenever they ache to discover the source of the roars or the light, they chug down the wine to forget what's denied to them. To numb their futile desires.

"Why do we do this? Why are we so willingly held captive?", they ask themselves then. But little do they attempt to look for an answer.

Until, one day, one of the aliens drops his tools, and looks in the direction of the gushing roars. He can't ignore the feeling that they might be beckoning to him. He struggles to turn his back on the calling. At that moment, a dim light starts burning within him. He reaches for the wine urn, to put off feelings of desire, as he has always done; but he stops himself.

The light begins to spread to the rest of his body, making him feel alive. Invincible.

Possessed, he kicks the urn away, and watches as it rolls on to its untimely death. For once, he does not want to succumb to the laws of the forest.

Burning thus, from head to toe, he walks towards his calling for months. He starves. He struggles. He regrets ever breaking away from the routine he was accustomed to. But he goes on.

One day, the unbelievable happens. His feet sink into a soft blanket of sand, and the air smells of salt. He walks on till cold water bathes his feet. The waves caress him, as if to console him. In that moment, he drops to his knees. With his head buried in his hands, he weeps.

"Why had he kept himself away from this for so long?", he thinks.

The first deserter of the system." Tej finishes.

STILL YESTERDAY
10:30 pm

He is no longer standing. He got up from the chair when he began to speak of the fire that burned within the stupid alien that discovered the Sea. He enacted the whole part with such pride, I had to crawl back into my hiding to pull myself together.

"I have kept my dreams waiting for too long. I should go after them. So what, if I starve? So what, if I struggle? If the path is going to lead me to the Sea that can make my life meaningful, I think I ought to just go! What do you say?", he asks.

A question for me. This is my chance to take back control. If I do not, this will be the end of me. Sighing, I crawl from under his bed, thinking of the things I could tell him, in order to make him change his mind.

I have been going on without introducing myself, have I?

I am the monster under his bed. The one that children say they see and good old parents do not believe.

Tej found me when I could barely stand on my own feet. When my family had failed to survive in a house where people seldom frowned.

Tej's parents laughed and laughed and they laughed. And my parents shrank and shrank, till they disappeared forever.

Alone, and starving, I was trembling under Tej's bed. I was moments away from meeting the same end as my family when a then 16-year-old Tej mumbled something about not being enough. That was enough for *me* to crawl out of my hiding and make my way to him.

He needed me. Only I could validate his feelings. I told him he was not wrong, and that every single thing he believed himself to be, was not far from the truth. And then, in that instance, an overwhelming feeling took over me. I was no longer starving. I was served a feast. A fear-feast. I went on telling him stories. I went on feeding off his fear. I went on growing. 13 years later, today, I can barely fit under his bed.

I am the monster under his bed. I am the narrator in his life. I am the master of the living, breathing puppet, Tej.

YESTERDAY
11:15 pm

Now, to address the problem in hand, I look him in the eye. I have got to get rid of all that the meaningless play and the thick-headed aliens have fed him with. It is unbelievable how years of effort can come undone in *one* evening. Casting my doubts aside, I hurl his worst fears at him, without holding back.

Straining my memory, I think of the numerous instances from his past that he dreads even today. But unlike other days, he is not wincing. He is staring at me blankly. Then, just like that, he falls asleep. His shoes are still on; so are the clothes from his day job. He has not a worry in the world as he sleeps. I am terrified. This can't be the end of me.

I climb onto his chest, singing to him songs of the agony he has witnessed. I whisper stories of his loss.

"Your father, he sure laughed a lot for an artist whose paintings barely sold. He wouldn't part ways with his art, no matter what life threw at him, he used to say. He lived through torn pants and broken chairs, hoping that one day, his art would be recognized. Then came desperation and death. Too soon for a man who was no older than 40, ha! They say art takes time to be recognized. But of what use is it if appreciation comes long after one's time? You know it does not help to put your heart above your head. You have wasted enough years in ambiguity. You have lost people on the go. Now is not the time to chase something that will not yield anything at all! Now is when you grit your teeth and make do with whatever life throws at you. Or, you will fail in life. You will fail so badly, you will have the whole world laughing in your face.", I press him down and scream at him.

MINUTES BEFORE NOW

2:45 am

I can't think of anything more to say. I am at a loss for words.

I sob loudly. My sobbing always broke him. He always followed suit, even when he was in deep sleep. Wet cheeks, and choked breathing. He was easy game.

But tonight, nothing seems to get to him. It is getting to me, instead. I sob louder, more for myself. I am beginning to feel stifled. Choked. Chained. I can't feel my limbs, and I am afraid they are no longer even there.

NOW
3:07 am

The memory film…it is glitching again. I can't seem to see anything anymore. Everything is a blur and I have to struggle to focus on his worriless face as I…

FEW HOURS LATER

10:30 am

I am Tej, a 29-year-old ventriloquist *and* a salesman. I had the best sleep, in ages. I am heading for work, and there is something different about today. My clothes and shoes feel larger. They seem to fit better. And my hands aren't as sweaty. I wonder if it is the weather. Whatever it is, I feel good.

"Say what, Peppy? Are you ready to throw yet another fabulous show? Are you? Then we will head to the rehearsals...We have dreams to make true, after all!".

Talking about dreams, I had a crazy one last night.

Come to think of it, I am not sure if it was just a dream. But I was looking into the mirror, and a huge raven-coloured blob loomed behind me. We were in a conversation. What we spoke of, I am unable to remember now. But it was packed with sobs and screams.

I remember feeling weak in my knees. My chest hurt, and I found it hard to breathe. But within the mirror, I did not look distressed. Instead, I saw myself smiling. Soon, the screams became distant as the blob itself began to shrink. Then there was nothing. It was just me and my reflection. I was relieved.

It felt like a sweet victory. Victory in what, I do not know.

But it sure feels like I am getting back in touch with the world, after ages. It feels like I have found my voice again.

2

The Worm

Once upon a windy time, a worm flew and fell onto a thorny bush. It yelped in pain at the unfortunate turn of events. How prickly the thorns were. Oh, how miserable its life was!

A snail that was on its way out, had witnessed the worm's fall. But there was nothing it could do to protect the worm. So, shaking its head sympathetically, it had left.

Weeks later, when the snail came back, it stopped by the bush, shocked. The worm was still where it had fallen. It had remained there, in pain, feeding on whatever little came its way.

Shaking its head in disbelief, the snail asked the worm, "You fell there by accident, but why are you not getting out of it?"

The worm replied, "I don't know where to go."

"But can't you figure that out once you step out of the bush? Look at yourself, bloody and wounded!", the snail exclaimed.

"If I step out of this, where will I go next?", the worm asked meekly.

Before the snail could answer, the worm had breathed its last.

"If one were to make their move only after knowing fully well where they would land, I wonder how they would land in a thorny bush…", the snail said out loud, to no one in particular.

3

A Deal With an Albino Pigeon

THE WIFE

I have lost count of the number of days I have been here. I am starting to feel that perhaps there's no meaning to my existence. I stand by the door to my cottage, and wait as I have, every morning, ever since I came here. The mailman comes pedaling with sacks of parcels and letters. He stops his vehicle outside my door as he always has. My hopes go up as they always do. Perhaps, I too will finally receive something today.

He brings out a writing pad from within his coat, and starts calling out names of my neighbours. One by one, they step forward and collect their possessions with glee. Some have received letters, while some, bouquets; some have gotten cakes, while some, stuffed toys. Everyone has received something, but for me. I stand by the door watching the mailman leave after nodding at me sympathetically. It's a daily affair.

I get back into the cottage, and lock the door behind me. Setting the fluffy white cushions right, I sit on the bright pink couch. Everything in this cottage, I specifically chose to my taste. I will be living here for God knows how long. I might as well do it in a grand fashion. That's why, a huge chandelier hangs in the middle of the room. That's why, the windows are dressed in regal velvet curtains. That's why I have a table for four in my dining room, although it's only me every day.

But what haunts me is that, in the entirety of this cottage, there's not a thing in memory of my family. There's no proof of their existence, within this cottage at least. The only way I know that they are real is through the constant hammering reminders of their absence, within my heart.

I made one friend here in all this time. I used to visit her cottage every time I missed home.

She was 60, and had stuffed toys that belonged to her grandchildren, sitting proudly on an otherwise empty showcase. She had letters and photographs from her family plastered on the walls. Any time I visited, her cottage smelt of fresh daisies…or lilies…or roses. Any time. Memories and traces of her family's existence breathed life into her desolate cottage. Life that can't be sensed inside my palatial home.

The woman is not here anymore. She received a notice a while ago, and has long vacated.

For me, there are no means to escape. And that makes matters difficult. I have neither received the notice, nor have I received keepsakes.

It has been four years since I left my family to come here. It was a choice I made after carefully considering every aspect of our lives. But it should not be as bad as to not receive any news on their lives afterwards, should it? Every passing minute in the last four years, I have ached to know how my children are doing. I have no access to their lives.

My daughters…they are twins. They were not… keeping healthy… when I last saw them. Do I not deserve to know if they are dead or alive? I won't ask for much. Just a letter that tells me that they are breathing. Even if they are not.

Four years ago, they were seven years old. Now, they must be 11. But I have trouble imagining them being any older than 7. My fears mock me. *Do you really think they survived? You think they are breathing now, as you dare to imagine their happy lives?* I can't fight these questions; I can't brush them aside. I surrender to them.

Their faces will soon disappear from my mind, and I will have nothing real to hold on to. The thought makes me sick in the stomach.

I still remember the day I first met my husband. A boy of 18, he had left his hometown in search of work.

I was all of 15. I was on a tram. He was sitting across from me, fidgeting; an open book even then. He had left his town because he could not bear to stay under the same roof as his parents, he told me with distaste. We got to talking during and long after our tram journey. We stood on the road eager to tell each other everything that there was to tell. His stories made me think that it was not too bad I was an orphan.

That evening, he came with me to the orphanage for a place to stay at as he searched for work. He offered to run errands, and help with chores. Long after he found a job, he continued to live there; he continued to help out at the orphanage, outside of his work hours. For my sake.

So, long after I turned 18, I too continued to live in the orphanage. Offering teaching assistance to the children at the center, I continued to study as I worked. For his sake.

I was 21 and he was 24, when we finally left the orphanage. We got married and moved into a small house. The house became our home. And our distaste for family life sobered down. Why, we fell in love with it.

We lived for each other at first.

Then, we had two beautiful girls whom we doted on.

We lived for each other, and them.

We had to work hard, for neither of us made big money. But we were happy…at least, I think so.

But today, I am on the verge of forgetting their faces. I wonder if they are dead or alive.

Selfishness. Greed. Hopeless hopefulness. They can change lives for the worst. Like they did, mine.

Was I right to do what I did? It does not matter now.

Wrapping a shawl around my neck, I step out of the door. It's chilly. I see white all around me. Too early to be snowing, but snow it does.

Try as I might, I can't think of an alternate solution for the catastrophe that came knocking at our door, four years ago. After all this time, I still feel that my running away was the only meaningful solution to it. Whether it worked or not is the one thing I would like to know. I would like to know if my daughters survived the mishap. Blinking away the stinging tears, I walk around my neighborhood.

THE HUSBAND

A run-down house that seems to have seen only the worst of mankind, stands in front of me. It's slightly slanted. I can tell the kids that I chose this place because it bears an uncanny resemblance to the Leaning Tower of Pisa. That would be my 107th lie to them; all because of my poor choices in life. Nothing is more depressing than having to lie to your own children, that much I can tell you.

My daughters are 11. They are twins. I once had a wife who protected the family with her bear hug.

But there was only so much she could also take. She was born for the bigger life where she sat idly all day, she told me when she had decided to leave. She was born to be dressed in fine silks and pearls. She could not go on living in nothingness, she told me. She could try, for the sake of our children, and for the sake of our years of love. But if things never got better, she would begin to hate the family that pushed her into compromising everything she once dreamt of, she said.

Or…had she said so at all? I can't draw a line between reality and my imagination now, after all these years.

All I know for sure is that four years ago, one night, careful not to wake the children up, she was gone. There were no traces of her anywhere. I did not know how to stop her. I could not bring myself to tell her that she could stay home all day. I knew I could not afford that.

I let her go.

Or, had I? I can't remember if I saw her leave. Because I wouldn't have let her, if I had.

Towards the time of her leaving, she barely spoke to me. She was aloof. She left early every morning, and was out late. She looked lost and miserable. I had never seen her like that before. Being unable to do something about it drove me insane. I remember asking her too many times, even for my liking, if she was unhappy with me. The more she said that she was not, the more I found myself believing that maybe, she was. That killed me.

Back then, I spent most of my days time-travelling. I could not beat the feeling that history was going to repeat itself. Or that it already had begun its replay.

And whenever I traveled back in time, I was not a father of two. Nor was I, a worried husband. I became the 11-year-old boy who couldn't put two and two together, again.

I say eleven for that was the last time I had felt as lost as I had in the month of my wife's disappearance.

One day when I was 11, I saw a pair of anklets falling out of Appa's* pillow case as I wrestled with it. It was a tangled, jingling mess. I picked the shining silver ornaments and looked at them eagerly. They were brand new! He had

* Father

perhaps bought it for Amma*, whose birthday was around the corner, I thought. Untangling them, I slid the anklets down the opening of the pillow case again. I felt like I had been let in on a secret. I couldn't help blushing every time I saw Amma or Appa. It was a beautiful feeling.

But three days after Amma's birthday, there still were no signs of anklets on her legs. Had Appa forgotten to give them to her amidst all his work? I remember a glimpse of my sulking face as I walked past the mirror on their bee-row. Surveying the surroundings, I slid my hand into his pillow case. There were no jingles. No anklets. Nothing inside.

I never brought it up to Amma or Appa.

Months passed, and I found another piece of jewelry in the same pillow case. Again, there were no signs of the jewel on Amma. Weeks later, one evening, when I found the pillowcase emptied of its contents yet again, I rushed out of the house. Feeling let down and confused, I sobbed to myself.

It was not until three years later that I began to put two and two together.

Receipts for clothes and such snuck in his books. Torn movie tickets in his pants' pockets. Long absences labelled work. Nights away that were termed 'last minute meets' with friends. Appa was with another woman. I was 15 when I saw them together. I was 15 when I was forced to see the reality for what it was.

I spent hours debating whether or not to tell Amma. She did too much work, even for a wife whose

---

* Mother

husband was no cheat. She was a devoted wife. Or so, I thought.

It was when I disclosed the gnawing secret to her, that I realized she was a *conditional* devout.

"I know…I know. That's how life is. Be grateful we will have no dearth of money here. Life is difficult outside!", she had said. It irked me.

The happenings in our house bore such loud similarities to the soap operas my mother watched on her TV, it was suffocating. Pretense, it was too much to bear.

When I turned 18, I turned a blind eye to all that happened within those walls, and decided to move out. I would work hard. I would support the family financially as a responsible son must. But I would have nothing more to do with them, I swore.

So, when my wife, the one who made me want to have a family again, left us, I spiraled into insane despair.

I struggled, and still do, to not think of my wife and I as the replica of my own parents. While they are no more in this world, the bitter aftertaste that they left behind, continues to wreak havoc in my mind.

It started the day my wife left: my lies to my children. I lied to keep them away from the harsh reality of our lives. They need not learn to brace storms so young. So, when I bring them to this house tomorrow, I will tell them the 107th lie – the one about the Leaning Tower of Pisa.

Inside, the house is not all that bad, thank goodness. A day's cleaning will make it eligible for family living. That's why I am a day early. I will fix the house and then bring my children here. We might not have to live here for long. In fact, I hope desperately that one of the consequences of our being in this house, will be that poverty leaves us forever.

A month before she disappeared, my wife suddenly decided to give up on her job. And I gave up on mine a month after she left, in order to discover the mystery that's my wife's disappearance. Where could she have gone?

By profession, I am a driver now. I do not own a car. I work for a man who has a host of cars. I earn enough to lead a bachelor's life – just me. Alas, I am no bachelor. With two children to provide for, matters are difficult. I can barely afford their education. I could take more trips, and earn more. But then I would not be able to give them the attention I can now.

That's where the move to this house comes into play.

I have, I think, identified the cause of my problems. There was not a single bird around our previous apartment. I had never seen one. That's a cause for worry, isn't it? There are a lot of birds in this locality. Plenty. There are both white birds and black birds. And double the bird poop. *When birds poo on you, you have a lucky day!* That's what they say. My fleeting thoughts, these days, are all like this one. They won't make all that sense.

But if you ask me, I am happy to have thoughts at all, at this point.

I climb the rusty iron stairs to the terrace, careful not to hold the railing. Once there, I see it's a long stretch of flooring, with no walls. None. I spot a dove sitting on a ledge, and my immediate instinct is to clap my hands eight times. That's what an old grandmother in the orphanage had asked me to do. I was talking to her when a dove flew by. She urged me to clap and make a wish immediately. Doves grant your wishes for anything new, if they are genuine, she told me.

I make my wishes now, all of them for my children, before the disinterested dove flies away.

But this is still not the main reason I am here.

I am here because I received intel on an Albino pigeon. You must know about the Albino Pigeons for their lore is sung far and wide. They are said to be part of a jury that helps you exchange your life's reality with someone else's. No one knows the complete story, for it's a thing of great mystery. But I have my ears where they are needed, and I have made myself well aware of the workings of the jury. That's why I have decided to move to this house. That's also why I chose driving cars for a living. I could look for signs of those pigeons even as I worked.

The first time I got to know of this world was the first night I spent with my wife. I heard her talking to an Albino Pigeon in her sleep. She was asking questions to him. She did that a lot. In the last month that she was with us, she seemed to have made peace with those pigeons, for she kept thanking them. She was a strange woman. Funny all the more that there wasn't a single bird back where we lived, four years ago. I laughed at her obsession with the bird, but never asked her what that was all about.

After she left, however, I changed my mind about the pigeons. She was a woman of sense. Rarely did she do anything senseless. So, I took it seriously. I have spent every moment of my free time over the last four years unveiling the mystery behind the Albino Pigeons. That I have secretly hoped for news about my wife's whereabouts in this journey, is no secret. I have spoken to sources a plenty, and here I am today, waiting for an Albino Pigeon.

Spreading my kerchief on the ground, I sit down. I see no signs of the pigeon. It does not appear in front of anyone and everyone. Or, appear it may, but not speak. I have had to go here and there and everywhere, to get myself an appointment with the Albino Pigeon of this locality. He can't see very well, and therefore takes more time traveling, I heard. I look at my watch, it is past noon. I am struggling to keep awake, when the air around me suddenly feels cool. I shiver as I look at the Sun overhead. I hear a whoosh of the wind, and then a tired coo.

"Sorry about the delay. My eyesight troubles me these days", I hear from behind me. Startled, I turn around.

I see a white pigeon with pink eyes and a pink beak perched on the ground beside me. I had heard of the legend of the Albino Pigeons. But to see one in its skin speaking to me casually, is a lot to take in. I realize I was rather hoping to be stood-up by the Pigeon, so I could finally put an end to years of obsession, and get my life together. But the Pigeon is right in front of me. There's no going back. Not now.

I nod nervously.

"So, are we ready to go?", he asks. I nod again.

"Touch my tail, with your eyes closed", he says. I follow his instructions, without a word.

When I open my eyes, I am in a dingy hallway that has also somehow managed to be colourful. I see glowing tubes on the walls, and a chandelier hanging from the ceiling. I have heard that the Life Market is situated underground. This looks like it.

The Albino pigeon that brought me to the market, is sitting on the far end of the hallway, on a 3-seat panel. There are two more pigeons; one on either side of him. To be honest, I don't know which is which, now. Or *who* is *who.*

The jury looks at me, each of them wearing tied one-eyed spectacles that are bigger than their heads. Then, they ask me why I am here. I have to give them convincing answers to this upon which they will allow me to participate in the market. I clear my throat, ball my shivering fists, and speak.

"I want to change the reality of my family's life!", I state, giving equal attention to all of the three pigeons. I do not want to offend them.

"What reality?", they ask, in unison.

"My girls, they still wait for their mother who has abandoned them. They sulk. They cry. They are disinterested in everything. They are too young to accept the actual reality."

"What's the actual reality?"

"My wife walked out of the marriage and motherhood, four years ago. I am not sure why. We were good, really. But she left… for someone? She would not. Something? I can't arrive at a conclusion. But leave she did. Now, my children are living a different reality."

"Different reality?"

"You see, she was a loving mother. Yet, she walked out. Almost as if she didn't once think of the children. I didn't want the children to see *that* reality. It would have been too hard on them, knowing that she *chose* to leave. So, I built them a different reality, according to which their mother is in a faraway country, battling a life-threatening illness. You see, this way, I thought I could eventually tell them that the treatment had failed, and she had died. But it has been four years, and I realize I can't make peace with *that* reality."

The Albino Pigeons are starting to look annoyed. I hurriedly continue my story, before they want me seen out.

"I find it difficult to tell them that my wife, who might be alive in some part of the world, living a life she thought she deserved, is dead. It isn't easy to accept she will never be back with us, laughing and singing. But the children are shrinking into themselves every passing day. I see them waking up in the middle of the night, crying. They hold hands, and pray. They have not made friends at school. They do not read. They barely eat, you'd know if you saw them. Every time they ask me about her, I tell them she will be home soon, despite myself. I have made it impossible for them to break-free and live a normal life. I want their reality to become beautiful. Can I have someone else's reality instead?", I plead.

"So, you're here to exchange your reality with someone else's?"

"Yes sir. Please!", I say.

"Who told you that you could do anything like that?", the pigeons talk in unison again.

Confused, I stare at them.

"It's impossible. We do not do that here.", they say.

I feel defeated, and ask them what it is that they do.

"Don't you know? Your wife used it once!" they say, before explaining to me what the market does.

THE WIFE

Nights are the easiest. Because, I am exhausted and leave no room for thoughts. I fall asleep as soon as I close my eyes. Last night was the same.

Now, I carry on with my morning routine. I walk to the door like I did yesterday, and wait for the mailman. You could call this a futile habit. But when there's nothing else to look forward to in life, only routines like these can keep you going.

The mailman is on time. He stops in front of my cottage, pulls his list out, calls out names, hands over packages, nods at me sympathetically, and pedals away. I let out a long breath and walk back inside.

My daughters, back when I was with them, would take turns every night to sleep next to me. They even included my husband in the cycle. I got a chance to sleep next to every one of them. We were a team. But in the end, I had decided to play solo and run away with a truth they deserved to know. I had included not one of them; and guilt has eaten me ever since.

Selfishness. Greed. Hopeless hopefulness. They got the better of me. Was I right to do what I did? I did not have the time to think then. Now I have plenty of time, but no answers.

I am lost in thoughts when I hear a knock on the door. Nobody visits me. Ever. I am amused. When I open it, I find the mailman standing with a grin on his face.

"Seems like your folks left you a little something, after all!", he says.

Blood drains off my face. I can't breathe. I barely manage to nod at him before taking the letter he is offering. He pats my shoulder, and leaves. I really wish he would stay. It would be good to have company, just today.

Long after he is gone, I continue to stand there, pondering. I didn't see this coming. Deep down, I had prayed for this day to never come, although I spent my days pining for contact with them. I had prayed that they would never learn where I was. Because, knowing where I was would mean knowing why I left; of my mistakes, and poor choices that jeopardized their lives.

I want to cry. But I am unable to.

Not daring to look at the note in my hand, I shut the door tight. I sit on the unnecessarily pink couch, waiting for the contents of my stomach to settle. I should not have eaten this morning. Sighing, I peel the tape holding the letter together.

When I pull it open, pain shoots up every part of my body. It is his handwriting. My husband's. A gazillion memories flood my mind. I don't fight them.

"You. My love. What did I do to deserve you?
The children…are with me. I…"

The letter ends. Abruptly. The words are blotchy, and the paper fragile. Of course, he could not write the rest of it. The first flush of warm tears run down my cheeks. I do not wipe them for I know there will be plenty today. My girls are alive. My babies.

It had worked. My deal with the Albino pigeons had worked! Like they had promised it would. Gratitude overtakes grief, and I cry happy tears.

THE ALBINO PIGEON

The man who wished for his reality to be exchanged has left the market speechless. We are keen on promises, our network of officials. One thing we can't imagine doing is breaking a promise. With the man gone, knowing everything about the deal his wife made with us, I am hit by a deluge of doubts. Had I ever promised the woman to not reveal her deal? After enough contemplation, I know I have broken no promises.

I am worried for the man…the husband. He was not ready to know the story. Not yet.

But isn't that how reality works? It finds you at the most unexpected of times, and pulls you into a whirlpool of truths you can't get away from. The only way to survive it is to stop fighting it. You surrender. You surrender, and wait for the whirlpool to spit you out. This story, this reality, will heal him.

Four years ago, one rainy evening, I had returned from a meeting with a prospective client. I was hovering around, thinking through the events of the day, when I heard the sound of sliding sand. There was desperate scurrying. Somebody had fallen into the tunnel, but was not attempting to get out. When the scurrying stopped, I saw a woman climb out of the tunnel, into the market.

I flapped my wings to grab her attention. When she looked at me, I asked her why she was here. Her pale face froze. She seemed relieved.

Wiping her tears from earlier, she said she had been looking for me for the last seven years. I was stunned.

"Where were you all this while?", she asked authoritatively. Pretense of strength. She was crumbling, I could tell.

I did not have the time to answer her, for she shot another question my way.

"What is this place? What does it do? Tell me everything…", she pleaded.

"You are standing in what is called The Life Market. Here, humans gift their lives to fellow humans. They do so by granting their lifespan to those that they wish to. Some lend their span to their loved ones, while some donate theirs to the Span Bank when they come to terms with their harsh reality. The market is mostly active during noon. I am one of the jury members. The jury, they come into play when…you see, before humans go on and sell their span, they have to convince us - the jury. There are three of us here. You are required to give us concrete reasons which are thoroughly evaluated. All this done, you gain access to participate in the market.", I told her.

She burst into a loud sob. She wished to meet with the jury immediately. She wanted to participate in the market.

She began her story.

She had first heard of the Life Market from an old woman who ran the orphanage, whom she called Ajji. Ajji's sister did not believe in living long. So, when she turned 60, she had given her remaining years to Ajji who had a zest for life. That's how Ajji had lived to be a 103-year-old.*

This strange woman who was then a girl of 9, had found the idea fascinating. So much, that every time she saw an Albino Pigeon, she would try talking to it. If it talked back, it would mean it was one of the Jury. But for years, no Albino Pigeon had attempted to speak to her. Why, she was not once acknowledged by the beaked creatures.

One day, when she was five months pregnant, her doctor, who was also a friend from the orphanage, had told her that her twin babies would come with complications. Complications that could remain dormant, or could wake up and shorten their lives. They would not last long in this world then, she had said. She had suggested termination.

"You will be better off not… again…please.", she had advised. But the mother-to-be hadn't budged.

Only the previous night, her husband had looked into her eyes and said, "I don't know why, but I feel content. A feeling I have never had a chance to experience before. It's the babies, you know? They are going to change our lives! I swear on my very life that I will never let harm befall them. After their birth, I will live every moment of my life for them… and you!"

---

* Granny

Hysterical over the memory of her husband's promise, she had begged the doctor to remember the story of the Albino Pigeons they had heard together at the orphanage.

"This is our only chance at having them, you say. I will find a way to save them!", she pleaded.

Her arguments futile against the stubborn mother-to-be, the doctor was left with no choice but to accede with her pleading.

A month later, the pregnant woman began fearing the worst. The consequences of her decision could prove deadly. What if she did not have enough years to offer her children? Had she been selfish? She had. She spent every passing minute questioning her judgment. But there was nothing she could do about it anymore.

Months passed and she birthed two beautiful girls. Girls she knew she would happily give her life for. The husband, the wife, and the twins had a pleasant life together.

But as happy as she seemed on the outside, the mother's desperate search for the Albino Pigeon that could save her children proved futile every passing year. Every time she thought of the day when she would have to let go of her children, she shuddered, wept, and scolded herself for giving up so soon.

The girls seemed to grow up fine, she told me. But a week before she arrived at the Life Market, everything had come crumbling down. The doctor had told her that the twins' streak of luck had come to an end. Their dormant malady had woken up, to claim their lives. They had a year left, at most. They were only seven at the time.

Helpless, she had spent the whole week looking for Albino Pigeons during the day, and chasing doctors in the evening. She hoped to find a pigeon or a doctor who would tell her that it was all a giant misunderstanding; and that the children would be okay. But nobody did so. The verdict was final.

If her husband ever found out what she had done, she would forever be remembered as a despicable mother. She could not bear the thought of snatching everything he lived for from him!

On her way back home that evening, she was walking aimlessly, blinded by tears that would not stop. That's when she heard a flutter of wings. She blinked urgently, to get rid of the tears. She saw a peculiar looking Albino Pigeon - me. When I flew down the tunnel, she slid through the tunnel herself. Then, she stood before me throwing facts, and demanding a meeting with the jury.

When they came, she debated with them. She was elated at being told she had a long life ahead of her.

"You are 30. You could live to be 84. You can split the remainder of your 54 years between the two of them.", my colleague had said.

"27? What can they do with 27! I have 54. Why can't each of them have 54? They can live up to 62!", she argued. She wouldn't settle.

She gave us plenty of reasons, and arguments unasked for. When she had nothing more to say, she asked us to be fair, and walked away. A week later, I found her standing under a tree as it rained. I had a message to pass. The Jury had agreed.

A month from then, she could trade her span. She cried tears of joy.

Her last day here, she walked back into the market and made me promise that I would stick to the deal. Then, collapsing on to the floor, she quietly departed this life.

It was impulsive, one would say. Her decision. It was not.

THE HUSBAND

I have not slept since my conversation with the Albino Pigeon. I am convinced that my heart has crumbled into nothingness, inside my ribs. I am barely alive. I can't stop thinking about her carefully laid out plans over the month she last was with us. The meticulously established distance, in every aspect. Can one really do that for their family? I was not there for her in the end. I can't make peace with that.

Worse, she had no way to know if the deal had worked at all. What if it had been a bogus move? Was her sacrifice worth it? The torment. Would I have put myself through this?

I look at my daughters walking alongside me, their sad faces pale. They deserve a better life. They always have.

I have told them the reality. Not the reality involving the Albino Pigeons; but the one about their mother's existence in this world. That it's no more. I think I saw them sigh in relief.

"She is out of pain.", they mumbled, and nodded.

They have their mother's heart, after all.

A Month after my wife's disappearance, the doctor had called our residence, asking me to bring the children for routine tests. I had followed her instructions without a second thought. She was my wife's trusted friend, after all. When I had dropped in at the hospital again for the reports, the doctor had beamed.

"The monsters have gone back to their sleep! They won't be up for some time!", she had hugged me, teary-eyed.

I had been too preoccupied to ask her what she meant. All that mattered to me was knowing my children were doing okay. I was relieved. The cost of the relief, I did not know then.

My daughters and I walk to a grave with no name on it. It's for those who know not where their loved ones are sleeping. It was where I had left her a poor excuse for a letter, yesterday. But I wanted her to know.

Sitting by the cold stone, we place little tokens of love that we have brought for her. It has been four years of darkness for her. She deserves the world. Tears trickle down my face, but I don't wipe them off. My children will see me as I am.

Now that I have answers to all my questions, I have decided against moving to the crooked house. We are going back to our home; the one where her essence lingers. There, I will make up for the last four years. The lost four years.

I will stick to my end of the promise.

...

This woman. She was a fool in love.

THE WIFE

My cottage smells of flowers every day. I have photographs pinned to my walls. There are stuffed toys, and long letters. I read and reread them with a smile on my face. My cottage is brimming with life, with memories and keepsakes.

I will miss this place when I am gone. If I remember it, at all. Yesterday, I too received the notice. My long transit is coming to an end. I will soon forget the life I have lived in this birth. Until then, I will soak these memories up.

Everything turned out fine in the end, thanks to the Albino Pigeons.

4

The Monkey

Swinging from one tree to another, was a Traveller Monkey on the lookout for a home. He had toured through forests far and wide, and inspected trees so many. And yet, he had not found a place he could call home. Because, at every tree he stopped by, he heard a deafening din. A noise that seemed like a hundred voices screaming a hundred different things that the poor monkey could not comprehend. A noise which, he realized, did not haunt him much when he was on the move. It was when he paused that the din was the loudest. So, he became a perpetual traveller.

Swinging around all the time, sometimes here, then there, and then somewhere else, the Traveller Monkey had made a lot of friends. Everyone loved him, for he was the funniest! They would see him closing his ears and shrieking, every time he stopped by to inspect a new tree.

"Do you too hear voices on this tree?" he would laugh, while gazing at the other animals searchingly, hoping he was not the only one!

But thinking of it as another joke from this funny guy whom they had all heard of long before he even arrived by their tree, the tigers, the birds, and the snakes would bellow with laughter. And our Monkey would roll on the ground monkeying around. Deep within, his heart sank.

You see, he was losing it every day, confused at the voices that threatened him. Mocked him. Was he to never have a moment's peace? Why was it only him? To these questions, he had no answers.

One day, when he had had enough, he ran to the hilltop. Alas, even there the Monkey heard voices. He shut his ears tight, snuck his head between his knees and screamed; as if challenging the voices to beat him!

He screamed and he screamed, looking around in despair. But the voices would not go. It was at that moment that he realized they were within him. Not in the trees, nor the hills. They were inside him!

Angry, he stopped screaming and rushed to the edge of the cliff. Maybe the voices would stop being if he stopped being. Shutting his eyes tight, the monkey stood ready to jump, when a wise blue bird who understood his plight, spoke to him.

"Oh! I hear them too! The voices.", she said.

The Monkey looked up, teary eyed. "You do?"

"Oh, I sure do! They were loud, earlier, but now they are quieter! I shut them up. You see, they function together. But alone, they make no sense. So, I put every ounce of my strength into singling the voices out, and listening. They are just gibberish, and so quick to vanish! You too can make them go!", she said.

The Monkey, now bathing in his own tears, cried out a million thanks. Together, they walked back into the jungle, both of them determined: the Monkey, to make the voices fade; and the bird, to see him to it!

5

Hiraeth

January, 1983.

The clock strikes eight. Picking the plastic smiling face that serves as her bank account, Pari stuffs a note inside. When it does not go in, her own face breaks into a smile, and her missing tooth shows. The bank is full. She can finally begin her mission. The realization makes her incapable of breathing.

She stretches her frail arms and legs on her bed. Pulling her blanket over, she counts on her fingers how much she owes Appu. Appu is her only friend here.

When they had first decided on partnering up for the mission, he had told her that cutting open the plastic bank was not going to be easy. He had demanded some payment from her savings. He came up with a fair process to decide on the deserving pay, as he put it. The plan was to cut open the bank, shuffle the notes with his eyes shut tight, and pick two.

No matter how many times she tries counting, Pari can't guess how much she might have to give him. It does not matter if there comes a circumstance where she has to give up all of her savings for Appu's sake, she concludes. Because he has been the only light in her life for some time now.

As she gazes into the darkness, her mind trots towards the first day she met Appu.

Two years ago, he had walked into her room out of nowhere. He looked unbothered, while Pari gasped. He had casually questioned her about everything he could think of. He refused to move to the next till she responded with answers that *he* thought were valid. For a 7-year-old, he had looked rather authoritative. Unlike a timid Pari.

After rehearsing in her mind enough times, she had cleared her throat and asked him meekly, *"Who are you? What are you doing here?"*.

He had looked at her with laughing eyes and said, *"I won't tell. It's a secret!"*.

Seeing her looking only a little terrified, he had decided that a little more terror would do no harm. He had improvised.

"Okay, I will tell you. I am a thief, and I am here to steal everything in this room, including you!".

Before Pari had been able to respond, Abi barged into the room looking furious. She dragged away a sheepish Appu by his arm. Such a shame he couldn't tease Pari a little longer. Abi, the housemaid, had smiled at Pari and apologized for her son's behaviour. She assured her again and again that he was no thief.

"If she complains to our sir, you will never be allowed into this house…you know?", Abi's frantic exclamations could be heard as they walked down the hallway; they were accompanied by Appu's whistles.

After the chaos had subdued, Pari found herself smiling. She had had good company, although a questioning one, after a long time.

The next morning when she had woken up, she saw Appu waiting by her door, grinning. He had accompanied Abi since he was convinced there was a lot of exploring to do in Pari's house.

Pari had gladly welcomed the company, till she realized she had yet to wash up. Waving her hands frantically, she had asked him to wait outside. Having mimicked her to his heart's content, Appu ran away vrooming, with his hands in front of him as if riding a bike.

It was then that Pari came up with a mission Appu could help her with! That was how their friendship had begun. They had been inseparable ever since.

Abi gratefully approved of the company, for her son would pick up good manners from Pari.

Two years have passed, just like that. Pari beams.

Thinking of what lies ahead of them, she shivers with excitement. All the theories Appu has taught her, would soon become a practical possibility.

She simply hopes for his lessons to be right, for she has learnt them by heart. Thinking thus, she falls asleep. With a smile on her face, she looks no different from the plastic money bank that sits next to her.

Morning comes, and Appu barges into the room to see if the unthinkable has happened; and it has! He goes straight to the bedside table, picks up the smiling bank, and the small blade they had bought along with it.

Pari gasps, but remains quiet. He is 9 years old and is capable of using small blades, he assures her, as if reading her mind.

Following moments of tense silence, Appu shrieks. There, on the floor, is sprawled a bunch of notes. He shuffles the notes with his eyes shut, and picks two; just as he had stated he would. They add up to 70 and he is elated.

Putting the notes into his pocket, he stands watching as Pari counts on. Once she is done, she grins triumphantly at Appu who mirrors her expression. Looking at the wall-clock, she rushes to change out of her night clothes. They can't afford to waste a moment. They have places to be; and plans to execute.

An hour later, the duo is standing still, their eyes wandering around the store they have visited so many times in the past. The difference is that, this time, they are customers. Pari points to a small white bicycle with a backrest and training wheels. Appu disagrees, and points to bigger bicycles. *"Pick the one you like, Pari. We can add on the backrest and extra wheels to every cycle!"*, he says confidently.

An hour more has passed, and they are walking back home. To Appu's right is a new, blue coloured bicycle. Overwhelmed, they are speechless. All of their hard work in the garden had paid off. Their mission would soon begin.

Reaching home, they sit by the doorstep and examine their buy. The cycle has a backrest, a basket and training wheels. Pari nudges Appu to try it. She knows he is dying to. She does not have to say more, for he is already up, dusting his shorts.

He holds the bicycle as he would something holy, and climbs on. Waving at her, he takes off! Pari can't believe he is riding for the first time in his life. All his theories have turned out to be right, after all. She feels hopeful. When Appu comes back grinning, Pari is already nodding off. So, they decide to commence their first session the next day.

Dawn comes, and Pari is brimming with energy. Appu helps her sit on the bicycle and lets her be for a while. She has been waiting for this moment for so long! Holding the handles tight, she stares at the path ahead determinedly. When she is ready, she nods at Appu.

Weeks of falling down and getting back up follow; there are peals of laughter when she does fine, and tears, when she is unable to muster the strength to pedal.

Each morning, they walk out of the door with their faces as bright as the Sun; when evening comes, they drag their feet back inside, panting for breath. But there is progress. They make sure there is.

MARCH, 1983

The day finally comes when Pari must put everything that she has learned, to good use; along with all her hopes that she has guarded for months.

Wearing a bag across her chest and a helmet over her head, she walks towards the bicycle. Appu had helped her pack all that she would need on her journey: A water bottle, some food, glucose, and two small cards with addresses on it – one to their house here, and the other that would take her to her destination. She climbs on gingerly. Adjusting the helmet for one last time, she sets off. In the mirror, she sees Appu waving frantically.

"Come back soon, Pari!", he shouts. Her journey is going to be long. He prays for everything to go as planned.

Pari pedals slowly, but steadily. Hours have passed, she goes on unperturbed. Time is no problem for her. She notices everyone staring at her, as if wondering where someone her age is headed to, all alone. She hopes nobody recognizes her. If they did, they would take her back home. And her mission would remain incomplete. She sulks at the thought and rides with her head bent down. She will not let anyone see her.

She makes multiple stops. To eat when her stomach grumbles. To sip on glucose when her body begs for rest. To stretch her frail limbs. Sometimes, when she stops thus, she takes a little too long to get going again. But get going, she does.

The sun is over her head when she stops for directions, for one last time.

It has been six hours since she left home, and she is not far from her destination. Her heart is beating fast and her stomach is being funny. She wishes again that Appu had come with her. They would have laughed off the jitters together.

Trying her best to soothe her fluttering heart, she pedals on.

She comes to a screeching stop in front of an old house, and gapes at a tall, black gate. Pushing it open, she walks on.

Stairs. Three. She sighs. Climbing them with all the energy she has left, she rings the doorbell. She can no longer feel her legs, but that is of no concern to her.

Memories raid her mind as she waits by the door. She thinks of the day it was decided that Pari would live where she lives. Like a bird snatched away from its nest and sent into the unknown, she too had struggled to cope with her move. She hadn't complained. Because, her mother had always said that one must do what is best for the family.

Her train of thoughts is broken when the door creaks open. Standing on the other side, is an old man. His eyes are wide in amusement.

He smiles at her through tears that are determined to keep coming; like they have been waiting for this escape for years. A lonely mind isn't where their solace lay. So, they gush down his cheeks, afraid he might lock them in, again.

"Now, how did you come here?", he asks Pari who can't tear her stubborn eyes away from his face. Knowing she would choke on her words if she attempted to speak, she points to the road where her bicycle stands.

The man bellows with laughter, patting her helmet and shaking his head in disbelief. He holds her shoulders firmly and pulls her into an embrace.

"You should not be doing the sort of things you do, at 68, Pari!", he laughs.

Parvathi smiles through her tears as she clings on to her husband for the first time in four years.

Four years ago, a week before their younger son and his pregnant wife could move into their new house, tragedy had struck. His wife had died, leaving the young man broken. How could the parents let their son live all by himself then?

They had offered to move in with him. But he could afford the expenses for only one, he had confessed ashamedly. He had spent all of his life's savings in trying to keep his wife alive. Now he had nothing but hefty loans to pay off.

The older couple made no money of their own. They could not aid their sons financially, even if they wanted to. So, it was decided that Parvathi would stay with their younger son till he got better; and her husband, with the older.

What had to be a matter of months grew longer and longer, for her son only sunk deeper into his grief. So, nobody brought it up; the passing time, nor the pain of separation. Not Parvathi. Not her husband.

Parvathi had gone on living with her son, helping him in any way that she could. She cooked for him, and took care of the chores. Most important of all, she gave him the space he required. But giving him space meant isolating herself; for in that house lived only two lonely beings whose happiness lay in being with their companions. Companions who were out of reach.

Her son mourned his dead wife. Parvathi mourned her separation from her husband.

There were no buses that took her to their older son's house. Walking the distance seemed impossible. He too was always away at work. He too struggled to make ends meet. How could they expect him to take his father places?

She yearned for her husband every day, but did not know how to get to him without bothering her sons.

Months passed, and then years. The grief-stricken son had carved an indispensable place for himself at a renowned organization. Money became the least of his concerns.

He appointed a maid to ensure his mother no longer toiled. Parvathi, who had distracted herself with chores now had none.

He spoke about installing a telephone. That way, she could speak with anyone she wished to, he said. But that only made her lose hopes of ever living with her husband.

She had given up on seeing him again, until she met Appu two years ago!

Now looking at her husband, she smiles triumphantly.

"I don't think I can start back home today. Ring up our son's workplace and let him know so, will you? Tell him I will start before sunrise tomorrow.", she says, dragging her feet into the house.

"The next time, it is going to be you coming to me… It's time you too learnt to ride a cycle. Appu and I have worked hard, and our rose-garden is in full bloom these days. I have begun saving. So, you will have your cycle soon. You will ride all the way to our house, first. Then, when we are even, we can start meeting mid-way, okay? As often as we can…",

Her husband bellows with laughter. Pari smiles to herself, grateful she can still make him do that.

6

The Planter

Just when she was beginning to understand what plants were, a little girl once found a seed, and decided to plant it. She put it in a small mud pot, and kept it on the windowsill by her bed.

She gave it her all. Watering it carefully, making sure it wasn't too much or too less, she watched the seed grow into a plant. She had made that happen, and she was ecstatic!

The plant started growing bigger and bigger, and the pot got larger and larger. Soon, she was obsessed with it. She spent all her time nurturing it. Her days went in plucking out wilting brown leaves; and her nights, in suffocation, for she slept under the ever-fluttering leaves. But little did she know the reason.

Years passed before she realized that the plant gave her no flowers.

It had given her nothing at all.

In fact, it had taken all that she could give. Her time. Her obsessive caring. And... her room.

What started out on a windowsill, now occupied a large part of her room. What was she doing? She did not want to stop and think. She was used to the plant's presence in her room; and was unsure of her feelings if it were to disappear from her sight. So, she continued to shrink into a corner, to accommodate the plant which was now a tree.

Gone were the days of the pot. The little girl, now a woman, dug into the floor with her bare hands to give the tree its space. It pierced into the windows, and broke out of the roof. It spread out majestically, and the woman could only crouch in a corner.

The tree grew and it grew, the woman shrank and she shrank.

She could not go on. She wanted to give up. She strained her neck to get a view of the door. But the tree's trunk stood in the way, menacingly. Where the window once was, were now sturdy barks. She realized it was too late. She had no way out, none. She had to fell the tree.

Then on, she spent her days scraping the tree with bare hands; and the nights, nursing her wounds.

With a sinking heart, she realized that felling the tree would take her longer than it had for her to grow it.

7

The Man Who Was a Dinosaur

"I am attempting to write a story.

I have read hundreds of thousands of stories in my life.

Yet, I have struggled to even begin writing this one.

But this is a story I want to tell. So, I will have it written, no matter how long it takes. Time is no constraint for me. At least, that's what I would like to believe.

I will begin.

I used to be a librarian then; one of the few librarians in my days who *owned* the library. Those around me assumed I was forced into the business. But trust me when I tell you this: I could have gone anywhere in the world, if I wanted to. I *chose* the library life. It suited me well, I thought. I still think so.

The largest in our region, the library was an ancestral property brimming with books dating back to centuries ago. I stacked it with an equal number of contemporary books.

I read one book a day, without a struggle. Now, it's often natural for people to think that reading is something every librarian must do, to be able to assist the visitors with their book-hunt. But that was not why I read.

When I became capable of reading sentences, books became my companions. The only ones. Time flew when I read them. I went to bed every night anticipating a good story. Because, when dawn broke, mother would take me to the library with her. I lived for the occasional escape into worlds different from mine. I must emphasize, however, that this need to escape reality did not have anything to do with my own reality being unpleasant. Because it was not. I was indifferent to my place in the world.

My schedule could be used in schools to help explain the meaning of monotony.

I walked into the library at eight every morning and sat at the front desk, assisting visitors with their needs. When I was not catering to them, I would sit reading a book. My desk was by the fireplace which has been lit only once, since my taking over.

At noon, I locked the door to have my lunch. Well, not just to have my lunch. It was also when I read books that were off-limits to the visitors. They were books from hundreds of years ago, after all. Mother had told me so. Some of the visitors had requested to borrow those books, having seen me read them. I could not allow that. The books were delicate, and needed extra care. I had politely refused and stopped bringing them out in the presence of visitors.

That's when I started locking the library during lunch. For an hour every day, the door remained shut as I plunged into ancient text, stories and facts. When I was done, I would place the book safely back in the 'restricted' section, and reopen the library for visitors.

I was rather too austere with those books, I think now.

I stepped out of the library at eight every evening, and walked home as slowly as I could. I did not particularly enjoy being at home, because it meant having to interact with family. The human world, I found to be complicated. If I had to count the number of humans I got along with, I wouldn't even need all my fingers. Those around me hinted that my relation with worlds within my books, was a cause of my distaste for the real world. It could be so. I never agreed. I never disagreed.

I do not remember much of my life before I turned 6. In fact, I remember nothing at all. My memory only plays from when I was a shabby 6-year-old who refused to talk to his parents. My mother, who's no more now, was affectionate. She was the only being I could bear to talk to. Even to her, as far as my memory goes, I uttered my first words only when I was nine. My father, I think, never really liked me. He looked at me with eyes that said 'You are not supposed to be here!'. We never exchanged pleasantries. We never got along. And I was never bothered by that.

Although I was their only child, we were a family of eleven living in our mansion. Sisters and brothers, my father's, all lived with us.

World outside the mansion was alien to me because I never went to school. My cousins and I received home tuition. Then, they got into jobs of their choice and left home. I stayed back to work at the library.

When my parents left the world, they left me with the house, along with a family that lived in it; they also left me the library. I know it was my mother's doing.

That ancient building became my only safe haven in this unwelcoming world.

I am 80 today. It has been a long time since I last locked the door to my haven. Because, they burnt it. Someone who did not want the dinosaurs to take over Earth, found the library, and burnt it. That was the only time the fireplace was ever lit.

To give you more context, I will tell you all that happened that Sunday morning.

The library was at the mouth of the path to a dense forest. It was a two-storied building with books everywhere the eyes wandered. I will not go too much into describing the library itself. I will leave it to my reader's imagination. Your imagination.

During weekends, it was only past lunch that the crowd poured into the library. So, I had uninterrupted reading sessions. I was, I think, 52 then. I was unmarried. Always have been. I did not understand the workings of a marriage. The union of humans. But that does not, in any way, affect our story. I will park it aside, and tell you my views on it if we ever meet.

It was a Sunday morning. I was reading a book when I heard three knocks on the door that was already open. Annoyed at having to fetch the visitor, I walked to the doorway. Standing there was a strange-looking man in a brown tuxedo.

"Come in, please!", I nodded at him.

He followed me into the library.

He looked around the building longingly, and cleared his throat. I assumed he was new to the place, and had perhaps come in search of something. I asked him to sit down, pointing to the chair in front of me. He obliged, and continued to stare at me. He seemed familiar, but I could not tell why. He looked like he wanted to ask me something, but could not find the words for it. He placed his shaking hands on the table and attempted to speak. He failed. He sat like that for seven minutes before he got up, nodded at me, and walked away without a word.

He looked let down, and I did not know what to make of it. For months after that, the man continued to stay on my mind. Why had he come? What had he wanted? Why did he seem familiar? I knew not.

Years passed. I turned 57. Back then, time really flew.

One Sunday morning, as I sat at my desk reading a story about a pirate who had been kidnapped by a group of villagers, I heard three knocks on the door. Even before I walked to the entrance, I knew it was that eccentric man. How I knew so, if you ask me, I won't know what to tell. What I do know is that, an overwhelming feeling of familiarity took over me.

We librarians, we live for a good story. Something told me that this man would pull me into a fascinating world of stories. A world that would shake the very core of my being. When I got to the door, I found the same strange man in what seemed like the same brown tuxedo. The man nor his suit, had aged a day since our last encounter.

But something else about him had changed. He looked less forlorn and more hopeful as he followed me to the desk, pulled the chair, and sat down. I did not want to send him empty handed this time. I was still struggling to pick one from the many questions I had for him in my mind, when he spoke up.

"Do you have very old books? They told me you'd have very old books!", he said eagerly.

"I do have old books. But I am afraid that the access to older books might be restricted for visitors. What do you want to know about? I will see if those books are available for lending!", I said. I genuinely wanted to help him, in whatever way I could.

"Achlars. Any books about Achlars?", he asked, his face not hiding his anticipation.

I didn't know what Achlars was, so I shook my head. Asking him to wait at the desk, I headed to the restricted section first, for I didn't remember any visitors ever having picked a book on Achlars. There it was. A brown leather-bound book sat on the shelf. I was both relieved and dismayed on finding it. How could I let the man have this book? It was against the rules of my library. Yet, I picked it and walked down to the tuxedo man, all the while thinking of how I had never noticed the book before.

“I found one…”, I was saying, when his face lit up. He snatched the book from me and ran his hands over it fondly, indifferent to the dust on it. Looking at me with hope, he returned the book.

“I don’t read your tongue. Is this a story? Could you read the last chapter of it please?”, he asked.

Now, that was a strange request. In all my years as a librarian, I hadn’t once been asked to read out anything to anyone. I looked around. There were no visitors to attend to. So, I agreed.

I flipped past the contents of the book to what looked like the last chapter, and cleared my throat –

“Aini rolled from her hand-made mat to the mat of the woman next to her. The woman in turn pulled her closer, and wrapped her arms around the tiny figure. Aini felt safe. Fluttering birds perched on the trees around, and began calling her. Squinting at the rising Sun that shone through the chinks between the leaves and branches, Aini sat up smiling.

She ran to the grains-basket and threw two hands-full around, causing the birds to flock. She grabbed more grains and sat with her palms stretched out. She loved it when the birds ate off her palms.

When the beaked creatures chirped satisfactorily, she ran towards the stream. Slow down, everyone shouted. She paid no heed. She hopped over rocks in the stream and rushed towards the waterfalls. She slipped, more than once, and the viewers’ hearts skipped a beat every time she did so. As fearless as they were, the Achlars were scared for Aini's safety. She was their Queen, after all.

Standing under the ice-cold water gushing down the hills, she wished she could stay this way forever. Of all the places she had been to before, this forest felt like home. After her bath, she ran to the bottom of the hills, and began her climb on all fours. There she sat, drying her hair. They called her the 'Queen on the hilltop', for a reason.

These days, nobody allowed her to help with the chores. It was evident to everyone that she was growing weaker. They urged her to sit still and just be. They needed her wits more than her muscles, they told her. Her guidance was the one thing they could not do without when the time came for the Achlars to take over the world again. She sighed as she combed her wet hair with her fingers. How much longer would she have to stay put? How much longer would it be before the trees grew? There were responsibilities she shouldered that she could not turn away from. Yet, with every passing day, she feared she was not far from forgetting her purpose. The purpose that meant everything to her kind. She shuddered at the thought of leaving the Achlars to fend for themselves.

She gazed at the trees. They were still small. Still yet to grow. Could they talk? Did they talk? She did not hear them. But maybe, the trees heard each other. What would they talk about? She was lost in her thoughts, when the tribe called her. It was time to pray, and Achlars always prayed together.

She began her climb down the path when she heard screams of commotion. A giant flame had danced its way towards the tribe. A forest-fire. The scene in front of her eyes turned gore.

Shrill screams pierced through the forest as the Achlars struggled to put out the fire. Aini began to rush down the hills. But the burning elders begged her not to. Climbing back to the hilltop, she witnessed the massacre. There was nothing she could do, to save them. Tears streamed down her face as she watched them burn. Their cries of agony paralyzed her.

Before the fires became any bigger, the rains poured. The splattering drops saved the trees. Though they were half-burnt, they were still alive; they would make it. But her tribe had fallen.

Hours later, she walked towards their remains. There was no movement. There was no sound, but for rain drops falling on burnt leaves, trees, and bodies. She could not recognize anyone. It dawned on her that she was all alone in that huge forest.

Screaming in horror, she ran as fast as her feet would take her. In that moment, she forgot all about her purpose and was nothing more than an 8-year-old who had lost her family. Legend says that she ran and ran, till she turned into a younger child."

Having read it without a break, I gulped down a glass of water. My throat had become dry.

Sitting on the chair with his head on the desk, the man in the tuxedo was breathing heavily. He was seething in fury, it seemed. I waited for what seemed like all of eternity but had been no longer than a minute, when he sat up straight.

"Have you heard this story before?" he gazed at me searchingly.

I shook my head, confused. I barely understood the story, to begin with. He sighed.

"Can I take the book with me?", he asked.

I shook my head again. I could not break the rules. I was rather austere with the old books. The man nodded, and walked out of the library with a look that said, "You have let me down. Again.".

But behind that look, I could swear I saw a smile of victory.

As for me, I was feeling guilty, but incapable of changing my decision. One of the reasons why I hadn't wanted to give him the book was that it had kindled my curiosity. I had decided I would stay in the library all night and read the book, even as I read the story to the man. So, it remained with me.

Later that evening, with all the visitors gone, I locked the door and sat with the book.

It was a detailed description on the lives of Achlars. Many hundreds of years ago, a tribe of people called the Achlars had occupied a small part of a huge forest – the forest whose description aligned with the one behind my library. The Achlars had come to the forest seeking refuge and it had become their home. They lived there in harmony with the animals and birds around. They were all part of their family.

Their existence was a well-kept secret. Nothing scared the Achlars but being discovered before completing their mission. The night they arrived in the forest, they had been carrying saplings of the Achla trees with them. They planted them far and wide, and lay waiting as they carried on with their day.

The chapters of the book as they progressed, focussed on the Achla trees. The tribe worshipped the trees and guarded them with their lives. It wasn't clear to me why. Having read the book, I wished the man would stop by.

Weeks later, he did. He refused to enter the library, citing his muddy shoes and tuxedo. I could not tell what he was up to, but I knew he was having a tough time. He sat on the steps to the door. I sat next to him.

"I read the whole book!", I told him.

He did not respond.

"What's the deal with the trees?", I asked.

"What do you know about dinosaurs?", he asked in turn.

"Uh…they are reptiles that walked the earth… hundred million years ago, what about them?".

"Are they alive or gone?".

I was beginning to feel confused. What did the trees have to do with this?

"They are gone…for good!", I told him.

"What if I told you they were alive? That they are waiting to avenge their loss?"

"How can they be alive? They are extinct. What loss?"

"What if I told you the Earth belonged to the dinosaurs. Earth was meant to be home to the dinosaurs. What if I told you that human beings that have taken over this planet, do not belong here! What would you say then? Everything man knows about dinosaurs is a myth. False."

What was the man going on about? I stayed silent.

"Many millions of years ago, the celebrated human beings invaded our Earth. Their planet was overpouring... no air to breathe, no free inch of ground to stand on. Their eyes chanced upon Earth. Earth that was brimming with nothing but dinosaurs, and trees that birthed and nourished them – the Achla trees. Dinosaurs came to life from within those trees. Jet black, and gigantic, the roots of the trees spread far and wide.", he was stating, vehemently. My amusement could not be held back, and I snickered.

He looked me in the eyes and smiled at me sadly.

"I am a dinosaur, myself. You must believe me.", he said, pressing my arms.

I did not know what to say to that. The man in front of me, in a brown tuxedo, was a reptile that has long been extinct? I decided I would be better off away from him, for I could make no sense of anything he uttered. I got up and dusted my pants, expecting the man to get the hint and walk away. But he stayed on. He went on.

"There are many more dinosaurs that lay waiting to claim our planet back. When they came, the humans, they set fire to every Achla tree there was in sight. We fled. Well…most of us did. Some were lost. We could not be seen in our being. They would have us dead in no time, if they were to spot us. So, our leader morphed us into beings big and small. Some of us became birds, while some turned into sea animals. Some of us became insects many times smaller, while some turned into land animals.

As you might have already realized, some of us became humans too. Some were the planters, in the guise of humans – the Achlars. We went into hiding; and the humans took over our planet. They spread stories about dinosaurs that once walked their earth. About evolution. About what not. We ate nothing but the leaves of the Achla trees, did you know that? We were all plant-eaters. The Achlars went far and wide, to grow the groves again, only to be discovered and burnt! We have spent thousands of years looking for the last of the trees. The Achlars you read to me about, they were the last of the planters. They were guarding the trees for us.", he became quiet.

I was quite taken aback when I realized that I had sat back down, gazing at the man. I was spellbound.

"The trees were only half-burnt. While it's true that they can no longer serve our purpose by themselves, their fruits can. So, we wait for the day they will bestow their fruits upon us. We wait for the day we can sow the seeds, and plant the Achlas far and wide again. We will protect them at all cost!", he said.

I nodded, despite myself. You see, I didn't believe what he told me. But I did not brush the story aside either. I did not want to think too much into it. For this was the kind of story that could suck you in, and leave you stripped of everything.

"Can I have the book?", he asked. I refused, again, I am not sure why.

"Fine. But I do hope that the fact I have not aged since we first met 5 years ago, should tell you something.", he said.

I had been pondering about the same ever since he walked into the library weeks ago, asking for the book. He had not aged a day.

"They will find out the whereabouts of this book, and they will take it. Do not let them.", he told me warningly, as he got up and walked away, not turning once.

Life went back to being normal after he left. But I could not stop thinking of him. No matter how hard I tried to stay away from the story, I could not. Every living creature I chanced upon, including lizards around our home and worms in our garden, reminded me of the man who said he was a dinosaur. Was it true that we were living in someone else's home, having kicked them away? I did not like the thought of it. I held debates and arguments in my head. On most days, I found myself hoping that the morphed dinosaurs would go back to their original forms. That the Achla trees would spread their gigantic black roots across the world, like they once had.

Months passed and I grew restless. One day, I found myself fully packed, gloves and all, standing at my doorway. I had decided to go see the forest for myself. The forest the book spoke of. I did not know what I expected to discover there, but I was brimming with strange hope. I took my first step towards the journey. A cool breeze caressed me, whispering endearingly into my ears. In the next moment, I saw the man in brown tuxedo standing with another in an orange tuxedo. They looked at me with a hopeful smile, their hands folded as if in prayer. Overwhelmed, I rushed back into the house, snapping out of the insane decision I had made on a sleepless night.

The next morning, when I walked into the library again, I was engulfed by a strange sense of comfort. The air was rich with life, it seemed. I sat at my desk, waiting for the first visitor of the day, when a group of insects buzzed their way into the library. They stayed a safe distance away from me and hovered in the air above, as if putting on a show. I gazed at them till they buzzed out of the door.

Sighing at all the bizarre happenings around me, I flipped open my book for the day and began reading, when a man in a blue tuxedo walked into the library. He cleared his throat and smiled at me, before walking to the shelves. Picking a book which he did not seem to have had even one look at, he sat down at one of the tables. He flipped through the pages absent-mindedly. An hour later, he walked away quietly, after nodding at me.

My time at the library became something that I looked forward to even more than I had before. The environment in and around the library was lively, to state the least. There were birds I had never seen before. There were reptiles that slithered in and out, as they pleased. Word spread, and my library began to be known as a marvel; a spot that had become nature's favourite. Many visitors walked in to witness it, men in tuxedos too walking amongst them. I began to feel at ease. I was accustomed to the plethora of life around me. It felt like home.

Many a time, the tuxedo men struck a conversation with me, talking about their lives.

They spoke to me of life before human invasion. They spoke to me of the leader they all looked up to. A leader who had long disappeared. A leader who had last morphed himself into Aini, from that leather-bound book. He had morphed himself a gazillion times as situations demanded, for the sake of their kind. He was on the verge of extinction and there was nothing the men in tuxedos could do about it. They told me stories that took me to a different age, and time.

Sometimes, they told me they were there to protect me. Other times, they talked about protecting the library. With every encounter, I found myself wishing they could go back to being the only creatures that walked the face of earth. The tuxedo men were the only beings other than mother whom I enjoyed associating with, after all.

One evening, when I was 60, I locked the door to the library and went back home. I did not know that it would be the last time I saw the beloved building. It was past midnight when there were loud knocks on my door. They told me my library was ablaze. I remember panting for breath, as I walked barefoot to witness the gore burning of wood. Perhaps they had found the book on Achlars; they had set the building on fire. I could not take this thought off my mind, and I became ill for months. As for the library, I never set it up again. I decided to embrace retirement.

As months went by and I regained my health, I took up gardening. Anything to keep myself busy.

When one is growing old, existential crisis is not as fleeting as it is when one's young. The feeling digs up a cosy corner in the mind, and stays on forever, growing bigger by the day.

Life went on, at a slow pace. There was nothing to look forward to, but fruits in my garden and the birds and beings that hovered around my house. I stopped reading altogether. Because reading reminded me of my burnt library, and that wasn't a welcome memory in my mind.

Now, a week ago, I pushed myself out of bed. After all this time, I was ready to see the library, courtesy of visions of tuxedo men that I saw everywhere around me.

I am 80. But the daily walks to the library, and back for all those years, have kept my legs in good shape. I think.

Holding on to my walking stick, I began my journey. The paths made me nostalgic. I had missed the routine. I stuck to my side of the lane, and took my time reaching the destination.

An hour had passed by the time I saw the grassy trail that would lead me to my locked library. But I could not walk further. My tired legs would not go on. I sat myself down slowly, leaning against the trunk of a big tree. I was getting my breathing on track when I heard birds chirping. It's natural for your eyes to follow the source of sound. That is what mine did.

My eyes landed on the back of a man standing in front of my library. He did not have to turn around for me to recognize him. The brown tuxedo gave him away. He was the first of many eccentric beings to have set foot into my library.

A bird sat on his shoulder, and two on his head. More birds hovered above him. There was a snake that had cosily spiralled around his arm. It sat hissing at the man as if they were in a serious conversation. Insects and worms drew circles in the air above and the ground below him. Suddenly, he turned around, and looked at the sky as if in prayer.

His face…it looked just like it had when I first saw him 35 years ago. He looked no older. As I gazed at him, I heard plops. There were fishes jumping up and down in the lake behind. They seemed restless. They had sensed the other morphed beings, perhaps!

Words and breath entangled in my throat, and I could get neither of them out. I shut my eyes tight, and opened them again, to see if I was really seeing all that I thought I was.

When I did so, I saw the man and his army of beings walking down the path I had been standing on only minutes ago. As he walked past, I saw saplings the colour of coal cradled in his palms. One, two, three…seven. There were seven Achla saplings.

I thought he had not noticed my presence. But he stopped walking, and turned towards me. He smiled as his eyes brimmed with tears.

"Master! The moment is here, master. You have got to wake up. We have found the saplings! We have done it. All you need to do now is remember who you are. You are not this loathsome human form that you have donned, master. Please shed it…please!", the man in the brown tuxedo pleaded with folding hands.

I won't deny it, I stopped breathing for a moment then. I did not understand a word he told me. The library might have burnt down, but I was still a librarian deep within. A man who never missed a good story.

So, I simply asked him, "If I am not this human, who am I?".

Looking at me in disbelief, he crumpled into a sobbing mess.

"We should not have allowed you to morph again. Not after Aini. We knew you were getting weaker. *You* knew you were getting weaker! We should not have let you put our mission above yourself. But I tried. That evening when you shed Aini's form and mustered every last bit of your strength to morph into another of these lesser beings as you ran, you collapsed by the library. You were a 3-year-old fighting for life. You could not breathe. It seemed to me then, that you were going to leave us! Do you not remember me screaming into your ears, master?", the tuxedo man cried.

I was shaking. Everything he said was alien to me. I wished, for his sake, that I would remember something. Anything. But I could not. I stood there gasping for breath, before I dragged my feet away from the man.

He did not follow.

A few days later, however…"

"Did he ever realize who he was?", the man in the orange tuxedo asked the one in brown.

Having read the whole story out loud, the man in the brown tuxedo could barely speak. He looked at their leader's diary with his unfinished story. He picked it and tucked it into his waist pocket. He could not let anyone read it.

"Did master never realize who he was?", the one in orange asked again, anxiously.

This time, the other shook his head in resignation.

"He would not have died, had he remembered even a glimpse of his past. Why, he would not have aged at all!"

It pained him to think that they would never see the leader of their clan in his true form ever again. Oh, how many times had they attempted to bring back his memory. To remind him he could go back to being the immortal majestic creature that he was. How could he have died a human?

"Deep within he would have known it all. He was helpless…weak.", said Orange. He hugged the leather-bound book on Achlars that they had spent so many months writing, to his chest.

The man in the brown tuxedo winced as he thought back to the day he had stood helplessly behind a tree watching the woman from the library rush to their pale-faced leader. He was fighting for his life. Without a second thought, she had wrapped him in her drapes and taken him home. She had breathed life into him. But he was no more the leader of their kind. He had become one of *them*.

The following dawn, when there were no human beings around the librarian's grave, hundreds of thousands of creatures surrounded him, silently weeping for their loss.

They would never see their leader again.

Nor would they ever walk the Earth in their true forms.

8

You and I

In a library, among many other books, there lay a red book with two stories; one called You, and the other called I.

You began from page one, and I, from the last. You and I were complete stories, having nothing to do with each other. Having never met, having never had the necessity to meet, they were unrelated.

Destiny, the librarian, sat at his desk while his child Fate wandered around the library, with his new found ink pot. Leaning against a trembling book-rack, Fate was wondering what to do, when the red book dropped down. Seeing it sprawled open on the floor and within his reach, Fate poured ink onto the pages in the middle.

Aghast, Destiny rushed from his seat and picked up the book, shaking his head at his son's restlessness. The pages soaked the ink up as it slowly spread both ways, leaving blotches on the conclusion of the stories. You and I were now meaninglessly incomplete.

Frantic, Destiny tore a few pages from the middle, before the ink could seep in any further; before it could wipe the stories out of existence.

With crucial parts having been erased from both the stories, he decided it was best to make You and I one. Sitting down at his desk, he began to read the stories. They made no sense. You and I were still unrelated...still incompatible. So, Destiny took it upon himself to fix it. He sat removing one page after the other. And every time he tore a sheet, he read the story from start to end.

Somewhere in the middle of both the stories, having torn yet another sheet, he read the book again.

He was awestruck.

He had brought You and I together to a point where the two had become one divine story. You and I flowed into each other beautifully; it felt right. A misty-eyed Destiny sat smiling at the turn of events, when he realized what he had done.

He had brought You and I to a point where they seemed complete, but could not be taken forward. No empty pages, no way ahead. The story could never be continued. He was not the Author, after all. Sighing, Destiny blamed his son. If not for Fate, You and I would not be where they are now.

Thus, despite effortlessly fitting in, You and I remained an unfinished story. A story beautifully incomplete.

9

The Dyad

A long time ago,
A bunch of people, who weren't people really,
Went about doing certain things in a certain wrong way.
The consequences were negligible, they thought.
Till, one by one, mortals from our world who were severely affected by the former's fallacy,
floated away into nothingness.
There was only one solution to undo the misdeed; to save the grief-stricken from their nomadic wandering.
And that was, to bring the Dyad to Earth. The Man-Tortoise Dyad.

THE SMITH

In a crumpled light brown shirt that must have once been cream, with buttons a few missing, he sat in his work place looking for a tool. He had just turned 55. It was half past five and he looked worn out. He had had a tiring day, his sunken eyes and creased forehead screamed.

Yet, he beamed when he finally found the plier. Before he could put it to use, Mani came to tell him about a job he had for him.

"A 10 days' work at Avadi. Nobody else can do it, and you know that. They will give you a room to stay. They say the food there is delicious, old man. I will pray to God that your dear daughter agrees to send you!", he laughed.

All through this speech, the smith only nodded, placing an occasional 'hmm' between his nods. He wasn't much of a talker, if the person involved in the conversation wasn't his daughter. The information which Mani brought, had been acknowledged. He would look into it later. For now, he had a job in hand. His last job for the day.

His customers sat in front of him, waiting for their new pendant to be accommodated into an already crowded necklace.

He was lost in his work, anybody could tell. And if you sat where those two customers did, you too would see his grey fingernails. It was not dirt that could be washed away later that evening. The colour was proof of years of toil. As if to give a cue, he hit the chain with the hammer, thrice in a row. Maybe, the hammer missed its aim sometimes; and maybe it hit the finger nails. A possibility. After three blows, he stopped and looked around him, frowning. Something was not right. Something had not been right since he left home in the morning. He did not know what.

He adjusted his posture, which he thought could be the culprit, and struck the chain again. Or so he thought. Because the chain slipped. Again. Confused, he blinked hard. Maybe, his eyesight that he solely depended on, was giving up on him. He shuddered.

That's why his daughter never let him stay outside after dark. She simply didn't trust him with himself. He was growing old, after all.

Moments passed, and down came the hammer, not missing its aim. He slid the pendant onto the necklace, sighing heavily as he did. They fit. Waving the necklace in front of the two, he smiled. He did not need words. A man of gestures.

When they got up to leave, he too stood up to straighten his crumpled clothes. He could not go home looking like that. His daughter would give him a sweet earful again. A few months ago, she had bought an iron box with the money she had earned by tutoring children every evening.

Since then, she never let him leave the house without his clothes neatly ironed.

The other day, when he had waved his tool-kit in front of her and laughed, she had tilted her head to one side and smiled sadly.

"No. You aren't just a smith. You're going to be an engineer's father. You work too hard. Wait till I start earning! Until then, your clothes will tell me if you've been overdoing it again!", she had said.

Both of them knew it would be long before she finished college. But neither seemed to worry about that. She dreamt big, and who was he to stop her?

She fussed over him so much that everybody who worked with him knew his darling daughter. She would come all the way to the store when he forgot his lunch at home. So, he had made a habit of checking thrice, to see if he had his lunch with him before he left. To every move of hers, he had to think of a counter move. But she always found a way around. She doted on him. Everyone working at the store did. He was a sweet old man who minded his business - a quality which few possessed these days.

Once he was convinced that he had fixed his still crumpled clothes, he got ready to leave.

"Where's your daughter? It has been a week since she has come here! Is she sick? That's the only thing that can keep her from coming to see you on her way back from college!", Mani teased him. He simply nodded. Mani was right. She had been sick for a week now.

He looked outside the window. It was about to get dark. His daughter had threatened to meet him midway on days he did not start home on time. Not like she would know if he did start late. But he still dared not. Because, what if she decided to come? It would take her a long, strenuous trip to the store. This, he did not like to even think of. Lifting his case, he fumbled for the bicycle key in his pant's pockets, and rushed to the staircase.

Hurriedly signing the employees' register at the exit, he smiled at Siva as he took the empty lunch box from him.

Siva was an old security guard who, unlike him, had no daughter to pack his lunch. He lived alone, and skipped cooking on most days. The restaurant was a long way from the store. Nearing 60, he found it tiring to walk the distance for lunch. So, he simply starved. Siva had only once mentioned this to the smith. The next day, he had received a lunch box from the jolly old man and it had continued all through the years.

"A new recipe today? Tell her it was tasty. I will miss your daughter's food when I retire in a few weeks...more than anything. I have been living off her cooking for the past 3 years!", Siva smiled. Squeezing his shoulders, the smith returned the smile.

Realizing that he was getting late, he ran to his bicycle. It was during this trip back home every day that he found himself lost in the memories of a distant past. The bicycle seemed to know its way, even as its owner sat pedalling in a daze.

It was half-past seven when he reached home. He was tired. But the prospect of talking to his daughter put a smile on his tired face. He looked forward to their kitchen talks, every night; although *she* did most of the talking. Climbing the stairs two at a time, he was soon standing in front of his house.

The door was shut, but his daughter's shoes weren't where they usually were. She must have picked them for a wash, he thought. Opening the door with his copy of the key, he went in looking for her. He wanted to tell her what Siva had told him about her food. He was impatient.

But she was not there. She was not in the bedroom, nor was she in the kitchen. She was nowhere. Sweating profusely, he worried. Where could she have gone when she was sick? She had never left the house at this hour in years, because she simply could not cope with the rocky roads. She had even promised him she would not. And yet, her shoes were gone.

Leaving the door ajar, he ran outside. He looked for her at the neighbours' and in the nearby streets. She wasn't there. Where was she then? He went home to see if she had returned. She had not.

That morning when he was leaving, she had told him his shirt buttons needed stitching. There was no point in ironing shirts with missing buttons, she had argued. She must have gone to buy them. This girl!

Gasping for breath, he rushed out again. Wandering the streets like a mad man, he refused to go home till he had found her.

He wanted to cry her name out, so she would hear him from wherever she was. She would come back to him and save him from his agony.

But how was he to do that?

He was mute!

He cursed himself, and ran around helplessly. She had taught him to read bits and pieces, but he was yet to learn to write. All he had with him was his sign language which would not, for the love of God, come to him then. He was trembling, and his nerves had long betrayed him. He roamed the streets thus, for two full days, with not a morsel of food. He went back home every once in a while, to see if she had returned. But his darling daughter was nowhere to be seen. He cried tears so many, his eyes grew heavy with every passing minute.

That morning, two days after she had gone missing, he gave up and returned home. His mind was blank. Traumatised, he was no longer aware of himself. Something told him she was gone forever; and he found himself believing the voice that said that. What was the point of his life now that his daughter was gone? He had nothing else to live for.

He opened the door to the balcony of their crumpling house that sat on the fourth floor of that crumpling building. He stood clinging to the railing. He imagined himself toppling down, falling head-first onto the ground. It soothed him. He would not be breaking anybody's heart, like his daughter had broken his. Mani would be disappointed in him. But he would understand.

He had no reason to live. So, he would not, he decided. But it was a struggle to jump; as much as it was a struggle to not jump. He wanted to die. But he simply wouldn't allow himself that death. In that moment, it seemed like his self was split into two squabbling halves. One that desperately wanted him to leave this world; and another, that begged him to stay. He didn't understand what was happening. He stood contemplating death for minutes. For hours. Then, shutting the door to the balcony, he simply walked back into the living room.

Sinking to the floor, he broke down inconsolably. He bawled. He bawled so loud, that even the heavens would have heard him cry.

The Turquoise Tortoise came out of his sand pit to see what the commotion was about. He moved slowly and steadily, clearing his throat. "Now, what is it?".

The man turned around, taken aback. There on the floor in his living room, coming from behind his couch, was a giant turquoise-coloured Tortoise. In the sign language he knew, he explained to the Tortoise that he was looking for his dear daughter.

"Now, why aren't you talking?!", the Tortoise snapped at the man, to which he gestured that he was dumb. The Tortoise bellowed with mocking laughter. Hurt, the man begged for trust.

"Please…", he said, and gasped as he spoke.

Astonished, he continued, "I am looking for my daughter. Where's she?".

The Tortoise, now losing his patience, spat at him, "Your daughter you say? Alright! Tell me the name of the daughter you're looking for with such anxiousness!".

The man stood still. His head ached as he tried to remember her name. What was it? Why did he not know it? He was terrified. What was happening? The world spun around him so fast; his feet were no more on the ground.

Moments later, having finally been slapped out of his vision of the sad smith, the man looked around and saw the Turquoise Tortoise. His Master.

He sighed. He had not been able to detach himself from his job today. At least, now he was in the safety of his house; away from the misery he dwelled in a moment ago. Away from that crumpling house. Away from the smith who was mad with grief.

"I was a smith this time, at the jewellers. A man of virtue. A mute, Master! He was so calm. There was not a worry in his mind. How did it so suddenly turn so upside-down, so as for him to want to end his life?", he spoke in a whisper.

Shaking his head, the Tortoise replied unenthusiastically, "You forget...again and again, that I see all you see. You see what you see, through me! Now wash the grief off your hands, and make supper. It's about time. You have no daughter that's going to make you dinner!".

"But they were beautiful. I hope the old man finds his daughter! Does he, Master? Will he?", Man sighed.

The Tortoise simply nodded. The man was beginning to be pulled into a web of emotions that he did not have the power to endure, he thought.

In no time, the man had set the table for two, and the duo dined together in silence, like they had for the past 149 years. They weren't fond of the humans' way of communication as much as they were, of their food. The man, who was simply called "Man", let his thoughts flow directly to the Turquoise Tortoise, who was called Master. Better to say, there simply was no thought on Man's mind that wasn't known to Master. No thought was meant to be solely his. If that were to happen, he would cease to exist.

However, having witnessed the mute smith struggling to convey what he intended to, Man was especially vocal today.

"A year left, from today. Then we'll be off!", he smiled at his master, thinking of the day the duo had first come here.

Given a house in the middle of nowhere, that was to serve their purpose during their time here, they had grown accustomed to it. Sipping the broth from his plate, the Tortoise nodded at Man.

"We have done a good job!".

"Who's it tomorrow, Master?", Man asked intrigued.

"When have I ever told you who it's going to be! You will see when you see! If I were you, I would not mull over the day's job once I know that it's done...not even for a minute; and I would not mull over tomorrow's job either!", the Tortoise replied in a drawl.

Soon, it was time to sleep. Man returned to his room, to his bed, having adopted the humans' way; and the Tortoise, back to his sandpit. Recently, Man had become unable to sleep as soon as he lay down. He, like most humans, had inculcated in himself the habit he could not afford to have. He had given way to thoughts.

Lying down staring into nothingness, he thought of the smith. Then, of the many lives he had lived during his time here. While he lived a life for not a moment after the job was done, he never knew what followed. How did they cope with their lives after he left? He had never known.

Tomorrow, he would wake up and live the life of, only Master knows, who! He had no complaints, for his was a satisfying job. He was helping in maintaining the balance crucial for the sustenance of this Universe. At least that's what the Black Bear had told them, when they were first summoned.

Hoping against hope for the smith to find his daughter, Man slipped into a slumber. Yet another sorrowful mortal awaits him, tomorrow. Yet another job.

THE GIRL

Sitting next to her calf, in the backyard, she peered into her earthen bank. It had been a few weeks since Thatha* started giving her a rupee every evening. He told her she could break the pot once it was full. But there was still room for more. Sighing, she kept it aside and stroked the calf.

She sat there lost in her thoughts, when she froze. There it was again. She was sure a glimpse of her parents had crossed her mind yet again. She shut her eyes in determination. Today, she would catch hold of that film in her mind.

13 years old now, she was tired of this little trouble of hers. No matter how much she tried, she simply could not remember what her parents looked like. Neither her grandma whom she called Paati**, nor her grandpa whom she called Thatha, had pictures of them. On some days, she would suddenly catch a glimpse of their faces in her fading memory, and try desperately to hold on to that. She would attempt to clean the image and sharpen it, so she could finally know who she looked like. That was all she wanted to know. A lot of people told her how much she looked like her mother. Then, there was an equal number that said she looked like her father. The biggest mystery in her life thus far! She simply had to solve it.

---

* Grandpa

** Granny

Seeing her sitting still with her eyes shut, and the calf looking at her hopefully, Thatha chuckled and decided against disturbing her. She was attempting, yet again, to know what her parents had looked like. Parents who had walked out on her when she was only three; one to the right, and the other to the left. She knew it all. Paati had made sure she knew it all. Because she, for one, had never forgiven them. And yet, this strange child held no hostility towards them. She fostered no ill feelings towards any one at all. To her, everything was a story, and a happy one at that.

Slowly closing the door behind him, Thatha walked to his bicycle. It was Sunday. It was going to be a long day for him; he was already exhausted. But Sundays also meant more sales. Determined, he opened the lock to the rusted chain that held his bicycle in its place. Setting up his big box on the carrier, he tied a bunch of fluffy, pink cotton candies to it. They went on to sway from one side to the other, as the wind ordered. Seconds after he had opened the gate, the door flew open.

"Did you see the packaging? They are alright, aren't they?", she asked, doubtfully.

Last evening, when he came back from work, she was standing by the door. A matter of high importance awaited him, she said. She had a proposal. He worked too hard, and she was not helping at all, she said, looking guilty. She wanted to help him.

With a sad smile on his face, he said, "If only I had the money, you would now be in school. Studying. You would not have had the time to think of all this!".

But she was persistent, and did not give up till she had convinced him that she would, at any cost, help him out with this work. That was how they had struck the deal where henceforth, she would help pack the cotton candies in their packets, without flattening them.

Excited, and doubtful of her first day at work, she could not wait to hear from him now.

"Why, they look better than my packaging!", Thatha laughed.

She clasped her hands together and beamed. Soon he was off to work, while she hopped back into the house.

She settled down on the only chair in their modest house. With a quizzical expression on her face, she flipped through pages of a long notebook. This, she did for hours.

It was 4:00 pm, when she shut the book and hopped to the backyard to feed the calf. As the calf ate, she explained what had been bothering her lately. She told her story, swaying her free hand up and down. She looked worried, and the calf mimicked her feelings.

She didn't have siblings. In their neighbourhood, there wasn't a single girl child of her age. She had had friends in school, but she didn't know where they were now. So, the calf had turned into her confidante. A calf that Paati had left behind, for her sake. If only Paati were here.

While she was around, Paati had been her best friend. She told her all about everything she needed to know. She taught her to cook, stitch, and tidy up the house; although she never really let her do any of the chores.

"Why start so early? You will have to do all this someday, when you have a family of your own, with children who will be wide-mouthed, just like you. For now, you read your books. That's what makes us the happiest!", she would say. The girl obliged, by reading books which Thatha brought from the library nearby, for hours.

Days after she turned 10, on a Sunday, Paati and the girl sat at the kitchen to cook a snack. She was going to teach her how to make Murukku* - a snack she loved with all her heart.

With her little fingers spread apart, she held the milk packet that Paati had neatly cut open, on the floor. It was glistening with oil she had herself applied all over the packet. As she sat there holding it, Paati drew dough swirls with the press-grater. They were both laughing and snorting at the shapes when, suddenly, Paati took her doughy hands to her chest and clutched it tight. She gasped for breath, and winced in pain, looking helplessly at the girl who was watching her with wide eyes. Before the girl could gather her senses, before she could get up, Paati had collapsed on the floor. She had never woken up.

---

* A deep-fried crunchy snack common in South India.

It was evening when she collapsed; only moments before Thatha got back home from work. Seeing him breakdown, she had forgotten to even cry then. She didn't like Thatha crying. She had quietly stepped into Paati's shoes that night. Tidying up the kitchen, she cooked a meal for the two, and washed the vessels in the backyard. When she finally went to her cot, she realized with a heavy heart that Paati was not going to be there with them from tomorrow. At least, she had Thatha.

The next day, Thatha left early in the morning, along with a few men from their neighbourhood. They were taking Paati away, and she was not allowed to go. It was a place she shouldn't see, Thatha told her. She remained angry only for a few minutes. Then, she went inside and went about with her day. She ate. She read. She tidied up.

It was half past noon when, out of nowhere, a doubt the size of a mountain towered over her. Would Thatha come back at all? She stopped what she was doing, and rushed to the door, where she sat till the sun set. She waited for him to come back. She was afraid that even Thatha would leave forever. Because Paati and Thatha had been friends long before she was even born. She couldn't blame him even if he decided to go with her, could she? But that wouldn't be fair on her. She was only a child. How could she live with both of them gone? Where would she go, if he did not come back? She sat there shivering, thinking more than anything of how she would sleep alone in their empty house.

The sky had turned dark, and people in the street started going back to their homes. She told herself that Thatha would never come back. Confused, and afraid of the dark, she ran into the house, and shut the door tight.

Just then, she heard the gate creaking. It was Thatha, wasn't it! She opened the door and saw him closing the gate behind him. In that moment, she was overwhelmed with gratitude towards the forlorn old man who had come back for her sake. He would be her only friend, she decided. Running to him, she hugged him tight and cried tears of joy. Then she grinned at him through her tears, tightly holding his hands, unable to tell him how happy she was. Even on a day like that. Thatha looked at the happy face that stood below. Life would try hard to rub that smile off her face. It had already begun! He shuddered on her behalf, thinking of the things she had yet to see once he too was forced to leave her.

Months after that, when she was on her summer vacation, one day, Thatha stood in front of her looking helpless. The same way Paati had looked at her, before she had collapsed. He was sweating all over. Just like Paati had.

Gritting her teeth, she balled her hands into fists and stood waiting for him to collapse on the floor.

Instead, he sighed and spoke. He told her that she would not be able to go to school for her 6th grade. He did not have the money. Teary-eyed, he struggled to get the words out. He promised her he would do everything to get her back to school at the earliest. She sighed in relief! He was not going to leave her.

She forgave him. But he simply didn't forgive himself. For two years after that, he seldom went far for work. He hated leaving her alone. But he also couldn't take her out in the sun, and let her suffer the fate that was destined for him. So, he decided, at no point in a day would he be any more than 20 minutes away from their house. Every day, he went home once, for lunch, and multiple other times, simply so.

As for her, she kept herself engaged. She cooked, and did the chores - most of which Thatha always managed to finish even before she was up...magically.

She spent the rest of her time reading. Thatha had not wanted her to waste her intelligence. He had gotten her second-hand copies of textbooks which students her age studied in school. While she understood some, she did not understand most of it. But read she would, again and again, hoping that one day she would understand it.

Seeing her struggling thus, one day, Thatha walked to an old teacher who lived down their lane. He had long retired. Thatha asked him if he could help his granddaughter. The man immediately agreed, and thus began her classes. All through the day, she would go through lessons in no particular order. She would mark her doubts. In the evening, she would hop down the road to her teacher whom she lovingly called 'sir'.

It was five in the evening; an hour had passed, as she sat reminiscing about the past. About Paati. She wondered if the cotton candies she had packed had been bought by someone. It was her first job, and she ached to be good at it. She would have to wait for Thatha to come home, to receive feedback.

The calf nuzzled against her face having eaten to its heart's content. Stroking its head, she got up to leave for her class. She packed her books in a plastic bag, locked the door to their house, and started down the street. It had been 3 years since she had gone to school. But she was doing okay, for she had the dear old man teaching her.

Besides, she liked the company of the old man, who gave her ideas for a new hobby every week. Of all the things she had been taught, she loved gardening the most. She liked how plants responded to the care, and popped a bud, or a leaf. It was the most real thing she had ever seen, and so she had decided to have gardening as her hobby. That was what she would tell anyone who asked her what her hobby was. But did hobby have to be something one practiced? Then she wouldn't be able to say that till she brought home a plant. She made a mental note to talk to Thatha about it, when he came back home.

Later that evening, having finished revising whatever had been taught for the day, she sat down to read a small story book. On Sundays, Thatha insisted they cook together although he came home late. So, she had all of the evening to herself.

She was flipping through the pages, when she felt a twisting ache in her stomach. Or was it her back? She had no idea where the pain came from. But she winced. It was the same pain that she had been telling the calf about, early this evening. She rolled around on her bed, trying to ease the pain. Suddenly, she noticed streaks of red on the bed cloth. She gasped. She did not understand what was happening. She looked around to see if there was red anywhere else.

It could not be blood. Nobody was hurt. She stood there confused. Confused if she had to worry about the ache in her stomach, or the streaks of red she found. She was still debating, when she felt something trickle down her thighs. It was blood again. Afraid, she rushed to the bathroom. There was something wrong with her health.

Cutting a towel into small pieces like she had seen Paati do, she stuffed them into her pants. If only Paati had been there, she thought!

That's when it struck her. She strained her memory to remember the best she could, of the days when Paati too had sneaked into the bathroom with strips of clothes. The same illness had been passed on to her, she concluded.

Then there was nothing to worry about. Paati had lived for so many years despite that. She decided she wouldn't tell Thatha and worry him. He did not have the money for a cure. Quickly tidying up the place, she forced herself to forget about illness she had discovered.

She was back to reading again. She had been at it for an hour, when she heard the gate creak. Thatha was home. She hoped again that her packaging had helped him sell more cotton candies! She hopped to the door, and opened it. Before she could wave at him, she heard the calf cry in agony. Something was wrong! She fled to the backyard to see the calf lying on the ground, shivering. There was white foam bubbling out of its mouth.

When she bent down to get a closer look at the calf, she saw a fat snake slithering away.

Seconds later, the cries stopped. She drew back, with her hands over her mouth. The calf had died. She sat there like that, with tears running down her face, for what seemed like hours. When she could finally move, she walked gingerly to Thatha. He would be devastated if he knew. It was all they had left of Paati, he always told her.

She walked to the living room and opened her mouth to call him, but stopped herself. There was no need to. There, lying on the middle of the floor, was Thatha himself. Motionless. For how long? She was panting for breath. Walking to him, she turned his face upwards, and saw the same white foam around his mouth. His eyeballs had rolled up, and he looked like Paati had, the day she left them. She felt blood drain from her body. She sat still, struggling to muster the courage to tell someone that Thatha must have died. There was no doubt. She somehow knew.

Suddenly, her shoulders turned heavy, like all of the world had been dropped on them. One after the other, everything that had happened since she was a child, towered over her menacingly, threatening to crash down on her.

She had not known her parents at all. But had heard of them quite a lot, from the neighbours who simply would not, for some reason, stop talking about them; and from the teachers who looked at her with pity. But she had had her grandparents who never let her feel their absence.

But then, when she was the happiest in life, her Paati had been snatched away. She had lost the only woman she had in her life. She had braved that storm for Thatha...with Thatha. She had had to quit school; but it was all for Thatha wasn't it? It did not matter. Then, the calf left her.

But even then, she had been sure she would get through the loss. Because, Thatha would be around. But now, with Thatha gone...what was she to do?

She felt a pain she had never felt before. It was too much for her to bear. What would she do all alone, in this world? She didn't want to be here. Unable to see through her tears, she ran blindly to the backyard, dashing into walls and vessels. Looking at the calf for one last time, she pushed herself to the well that stood there.

The well that had no water, served no purpose - she had often laughed. But today, that well would save her from the pain she felt tearing through her. Holding on to the rim that was crumbling down, she climbed on it and stood gingerly.

It was a struggle to jump; as much as it was a struggle to not jump. She wanted to die. But she simply wouldn't allow herself that death. In that moment, it seemed like her self was split into two squabbling halves. One that desperately wanted her to leave this world; and another, that begged her to stay. She didn't understand what was happening. She stood thus, for minutes. For hours. Then she simply came back to the living room, and shut the door to the backyard.

Sinking to the floor, she broke down, inconsolably. She bawled. She bawled so loud, that even the heavens could have heard her cry.

The Turquoise Tortoise came out of his sand pit, to see what all the commotion was about. Slowly and steadily, he moved, clearing his throat. "What is it again?".

The girl turned around, taken aback. There, on the floor, in their living room, coming from behind the couch, she saw a giant Turquoise Tortoise, through her tears. She tried finding a response to the Tortoise's question, but couldn't.

She stood still. Her head ached as she tried to think of a response. She was terrified. What was happening?

The world spun around her so fast. Her feet were no more on the ground.

Moments later, having been slapped out of his vision of the 13-year-old girl, Man looked around, and saw the Turquoise Tortoise. His Master.

He sighed. He had not been able to detach himself from his job, yet again. But now he was back home. Away from that small house. Away from the confused child who had to see so much grief, all at once.

"I was a 13-year-old today, Master!", he sighed.

The Tortoise stopped him right there. He could not allow Man to think of the mortals any further than he had already had. Man was in no position to be able to relive the miseries of the girl. He hadn't yet been able to let go of the smith from his previous job, after all.

After their dinner, Man went to bed. He was left alone with the thoughts he struggled to fight. He ached to know what happened to the smith yesterday and with that child, today. She had been so happy. Why did it become so difficult, all of a sudden? Man could only hope they would be saved.

He believed in the Black Bear. In the System. He remembered the story the Black Bear had told them.

A story he had told every Man-Tortoise dyad that had descended the Earth, and walked it for the next 150 years. The story behind their existence. The story of creation.

BLACK BEAR

Black Bear, who was in fact no bear at all, sat in the dark alley, looking every bit human. He was waiting impatiently for the Dyad to show up already.

Once a man himself, like the smith, Black Bear had been the first one to tamper with the 'balance of the Universe'. But it was no fault of his. He had been the first of his kind, to be subjected to inexplicable grief. He had seen so much of it, that he had resorted to taking his own life.

When he had gone to the Azure above, he had looked menacing, and had furiously hurled questions at the authority, earning him the name 'Black Bear'. He had asked them why he had had to live a life so cruel, when those around him bathed in joy. He had lived in the Azure ever since, among the Creators, and seen many grieving mortals getting trapped in the realm in between. They couldn't make it even to Azure. They remained lost.

So, Black Bear was sent back to Earth by the creators themselves, to first restore, and then sustain the balance. To say he took his job seriously, would still be trivialization.

So, he sat there that day, shaking his head at this Dyad who had the audacity to show up late. When they finally did come, with not so much as a greeting, he had begun his story. The story he told every Man-Tortoise dyad that had walked the Earth.

"Many million years ago in the Azure above, when the Creators first designed the countless souls that would serve this Universe for eternity, they had woven their stories with intricacy. Turning authors, they had sat down to write every second of the lives the souls would live. They had spent years creating the prototypes. The only touchstone of creation was that every soul's story comprised equal parts Grief and Joy. Equal parts black and white.

Every emotion that's known to exist, was sorted equally under the two; for every emotion was good, and every emotion was bad. There was fear that was good, that led one to do things that led to joy: the white. There was also fear that was bad, that led one to do things that led to grief: the black. The touchstone of creation thus, was for the souls to be an unbiased grey.

But legend says, once done with the core creation, the Authors passed on the job of further creation, to those next-in-line, while they left for another Universe. All that the subordinates had to do was carefully interweave stories originally created, to design a new soul - an amalgam of the countless souls already created by our Creators. A job so facile!

But be that as it may, those next-in-line were careless. Their amalgamation resulted in souls acquiring more or less of joy or grief, affecting the make-up. It was negligible, and even a blessing, when souls were bestowed with an excess of joy; but it was a disaster, a curse, when they were damned with an intolerable amount of grief.

Those ill-fated souls could not cope. No soul had been designed to withstand such grief, after all. As a result, as years went by, those cursed souls resorted to taking their lives, when the going got tougher than they could imagine. This self-destruction wasn't part of any story ever written. Our Creators were dismayed. Souls, the containers of stories, that they had so carefully designed were transcended way before the intended time, thereby leaving them lost in the world in-between. The balance was tampered with.

That was when, afraid that a lot more souls will be lost forever over a trivial fallacy, bringing this Universe to its doom, all of Azure concluded that they would send to Earth their last resort - the first Man-Tortoise Dyad.

Many thousands of years ago, the first Turquoise Tortoise descended to Earth, with Man sitting on His back. They were to serve for the next 150 years. Listen carefully to what I say next, for this is the purpose of your existence.

Before a mortal resorts to taking his life, Man, who lacks the ability to feel emotions, is sent to dwell in the soul of the mortal who's immersed in grief; He soaks up the intense agony which otherwise would force the mortal to throw away his life, to rid himself of the pain. When he is sure that the mortal has passed the moment of weakness, Man detaches himself from the soul and goes back to the Turquoise Tortoise, who closely monitors the passing of events through Man himself. While the mortal's grief is abated, he will still retain every memory of the moments that have passed. A mortal whose soul has once been touched by Man, may still resort to taking his life later on, for a different reason; when he will be saved again. But never will he go back to the instance he has once been saved from, for Man's healing is eternal. This is what the Creator's stratagem says.

As luck would have it, the only counter strike they had to the fiasco during the creation, was a success. Lives were saved. Souls were saved.

But I did not like it that the mortals had to endure a torturous life, to ensure they did not tamper with the balance of the universe. They had no reason to live with grief eating them from within. They were saved, only to be sent back to the hell they wanted to flee from; and it was not even their fault. I would never allow it. Thus, we concluded that we would save the cursed mortals, and also give them a reason to live.

We decided to make their paths cross with the fellow grief-stricken, giving them, in each other, a reason to live.

Ever since, a new Dyad descended to Earth every 150 years, to sustain the balance. Over the years, more than one Dyad were sent simultaneously, for the need rose. Now it's your turn. The two of you will help save souls, as many as you can. But Man, Beware. Towards the end of your time here, you will grow weaker, having had to live through years of intense pain. You will ache, when your mortal aches. You will find it hard to detach yourself from the soul, once the job is done. But you have not to worry, for the Tortoise will always be there to drag you out. You know where to find me, if you need me. But I hope it never comes to that".

Saying thus, Black Bear had bowed to the Dyad, and marked the end of their one-way conversation.

Having begun their journey years ago, they sure had come a long way. How many souls had been saved! And how many emotions endured. Man found himself thinking of the smith again. How bruised was his soul! Then he thought of the girl. How unfair life had been to her!

He had not been able to leave the mortal's soul yesterday. He had been carried away by the grief he had seen today. He was growing weaker, evidently. This was his last year, after all. He had been sucked into the darkness that dwelled within the souls.

But like Black Bear had told him, he had been saved by the Tortoise. But was the smith alright? What was the girl doing now? Thinking thus, Man went into a slumber.

THE SMITH AND THE GIRL

The next morning, an old man stood in front of his daughter's pyre. He still did not understand what had happened. He had seen her that morning, a few days ago. She had packed his lunch, and Siva's. Like every other day. When he had come back home, she was nowhere to be seen. It was on the third day, hours after he had returned home, that the police had walked into his house, asking him to go with them to recognize a certain body they had found alongside a pair of crushed crutches that lay under the bridge. He had gasped when they mentioned the crutches, and stood transfixed. He knew what awaited him, and he had to be allowed the time to brace himself before he followed them.

There, at the bridge not far away from his house, the man stood along with the police, looking at the scene below. Had she tumbled down? She wouldn't. Why, she never took the bridge at all. Something did not add up, but the man had no strength left to think. As if in response to his thoughts, one of the men cleared his throat and started.

"It'll, no doubt, be difficult to hear what I have to say. But we owe you the explanation, sir. We've been told that the accident occurred on the street your house is in. A group of drunk boys had crashed into the victim whom they suspected to have died instantly. They went through the trouble of picking her up, and tossing her off from over here, lest they are caught. They were thoroughly drunk, and do not remember much of what passed, at all. The camera took us through the happenings! We're really sorry! Would you like to go down?".

The man nodded, and followed them quietly. He was dead within.

He watched the pyre burn. Grief. To him, grief wasn't new. It had been his constant companion. Born mute, he had lost his parents when he was only 3. Grief had been there then. Having suffered enough at his caretaker's, he had fled to make a life of his own. Only 20, he had been alone, afraid and helpless. But he had survived. Why, he had been lucky enough to find love! But in his life, happy times never lasted. When he was 30, his wife of five years, who had been the only light in his life, had died giving birth to their daughter. Grief had been there through it all. But years later, when his daughter had lost a leg to a fall, for once, he had been grateful that she was still alive.

They had not let grief get into their lives then. Together, they had conquered it. The father and daughter had lived for each other ever since. Maybe that was what was wrong. Because it was grief that was meant to be by his side forever, after all. Not his daughter.

And after all this time, it had paved its way back into his life again. Sinking to the ground, he grabbed dirt in his fists and cried. He cried for the cursed life he had had to endure. A heart-wrenching cry. When he was finished, he got up, and headed home. He had a 10 days' job in hand. One that Mani had given him. He bathed longer that day, in an attempt to wash away his grief. Soon, he took his tool case, and pedalled to Avadi for the job that awaited him.

In a crumpled light brown shirt that must have once been cream, with buttons a few still missing, he sat in his work place. He had just turned 55. It was half past five, and he looked worn out, after a tiring day. Sunken eyes, a creased forehead, he looked older than he did a week ago.

His work for the day done, he got up and packed his belongings. There was no rush, for there was no one waiting for him. His clothes, still crumpled, he started back to the room that was to be his home for the next 10 days.

He pedalled absent-mindedly. When he turned around a corner, he nearly ran into a young girl with a tear-streaked face, and steered his bicycle away just in time.

She hadn't even noticed him. She looked like she had to get somewhere, but did not know where she was headed. She couldn't move. She dragged her feet and walked two steps. She gave up, and sat down on the pavement.

She did not have it in her to go on with her life, and she had her reasons. Her parents had long gone, then her Paati. Her calf had left her, then her Thatha. She did not want to be in that dark, empty house. Helpless, and confused, she looked around her, till her eyes met the man's. Turning back, he found himself cycling towards her. Her sad eyes beckoned to him.

He walked over to her and gestured that he was mute. She nodded, patting the spot next to her, asking him to sit down. Why, he reminded her so much of Thatha! His eyes, sad but honest. Even if he had not looked like Thatha, she would still have let him sit. She could not bear the loneliness any longer. The world was big and scary; and she was all alone.

The smith sat quietly, waiting for her to do the talking. She was troubled, he knew. Yet she wouldn't speak.

It was upon him to start the conversation. Slowly pulling out the newspaper he had tucked in his pocket, he opened it and then went about straightening the creases. When he was finally done, he flipped the pages till he found the picture of his daughter. Pointing to the news below it, the man looked away, his eyes gleaming with tears.

She read the article in silence. Looking at him through her teary eyes, she smiled sadly. Life had been unfair to him as well. As he folded the newspaper and tucked it into his pocket, the girl could not hold back anymore. Why was life so cruel to some?

Crying, she told him all that had happened to her recently, and all through the years. She told him how she had discovered she had the same illness as Paati, but couldn't ask her what to do about it, because she wasn't around.

The man looked at her sadly, remembering how his own daughter had struggled to grow up without a mother; without a woman in her life. His eyes blazed with anger towards fate that had pushed them towards lives so miserable.

When they had both calmed down, he got up and walked to his bicycle. With gestures miserably failing him yet again, he asked her if she would sit on the cycle's carrier. She nodded, and they left.

Just the way he had taken his daughter around.
Just the way her Thatha had taken her around.

"And in each other,
they will now find a reason to live"
– Azure, Black Bear, and the DYAD.

10

The Prisoners

In a faraway land, there once stood a prison which seemed calm from the outside. But captured within, lay a group of chaotic prisoners called Emotions; their only crime being their unintended usurpation of their owner's psyche. They did not walk; they rushed. They did not flow; they poured. They caused havoc whenever they showed up. Now, they craved to be let out.

Anger lay in one cell, scraping the walls with a weapon he had made with stones. He could break-out of the cell if he kept at it, he was sure. Grief lay in another cell, screaming his lungs out for liberation. He howled day and night.

Anxiety lay on all fours, drawing figures on the floor with his fingers. Figures of everything he had lost, and had yet to lose. He was ignorant of the world outside. Guilt ran haywire within his, not knowing what to do, or where to go. Dashing blindly into the walls over and over again, he was a bloody mess.

Many such prisoners lay captive in dark cells, all craving for an escape. The warden, who was called Brain, found it difficult to keep them at bay. So, he brought a box of pacifiers to help them cope. The pacifiers came in different forms.

He threw the first one into Anger's cell. A thick cloth and a box of colours. Anger spread the cloth wide open and glared at it. He splashed the liquids all over it, with all his wrath. Wildly. With every splash of colours, with every stroke, Anger became calmer. A wildly beautiful painting lay before him.

Brain walked to Grief and pushed in a pacifier. A potion that could turn screams into words. Grief began singing, letting out all that he felt. Tears streamed down his face as he sang. His painfully beautiful melody helped him soothe himself.

A book and a pen tumbled into Anxiety's cell. He grabbed them like a hungry man would, a pack of food. Ink flowed from the pen, onto the paper. And words poured out of him, making way for soulful poetry. Everything that he felt within him, took the shape of letters curved and bent. Anxiety felt lighter with every word he wrote.

Guilt was the recipient of a numbered mat. He hopped along in accordance with the numbering. Soon, his hands swayed in the air while his legs did wonders. He paid no heed to the numbers anymore. He danced endlessly that night, slow and mindless; but with order and grace. His lips curved into a smile.

Word about the warden's methods spread far and wide in the Land of Prisons; they were adopted by wardens across the world, to pacify their prisoners. As time went by, the prisoners felt no need to revolt. They began to channel all that they felt into what they had begun to collectively refer to as Art. They did not rush; they walked. They did not pour; they gently flowed.

And one day, Brain decided that they no longer needed to be kept locked.

They were liberated.

11

In a Purple Universe

NOW

I am standing in front of my door, looking for the key. I can't find it. Whether I am anxious that I can't find them, or I can't find them *because* I am anxious, I can't tell. I am late today. There's a feeling of doom that I can't brush aside. Is today going to mark the end of it all?

I have found the key, but holding it to the door seems impossible. My fingers are liquid, and the beating of my heart is deafening. When the door is finally open, I rush to my bedroom.

Pitch black.

I fumble around to get to the long window. Then, I scan my surroundings with my hands, till they are on the chair. I drag it to where I am, and sit. My breathing is heavier than ever. Minutes have passed when I finally thrust the window open.

I peer outside, to block everything in my view but for the window across the street. It's open. It's dark. I chase away the lump forming in my throat, as I search for the light switch.

The warmth of light hits my face. Then, like a mirror mimicking the act of the subject in front of it, the light in the room across the street turns on. Sitting by the window is a familiar silhouette. I shut my eyes tight. My heart beats so fast, I suspect a band of musicians inside. When I open my eyes again, the window is still open and the silhouette, still seated.

He had waited.

He picks up his violin, places his chin on it, and starts playing. I hear faint notes that are enough to set all of me on fire. My nerves jump about, and ice-cold blood gushes through my veins. The hair on my spine and limbs stands up. Goosebumps, even when all I hear is a bunch of disconnected notes that make it to my window from his.

Picking up my pencil, not wasting a moment, I pull out a sheet from the printer. I start scribbling on it.

Would it always be this way?
The closest we can get –
The coming together of
Your few notes and my string of words?
Will all of what's meant, ever reach our souls?
I…

For reasons unknown, my eyes sting. I am writing, striking, and writing again. The lead breaks. But I have lined up an array of pencils for moments like this. I know I can't afford to stop. I write on, as I stare longingly at the silhouette. I see his arms flailing in great frenzy. He can't seem to stop playing either.

It has been seven months since we met. Him and I. The word 'meeting' might be deemed unfit for our union which is yet to happen. It was earlier this year that I first saw him…or, his silhouette.

THEN

I never opened the windows, let alone the long one by the corner. I liked it quiet. I liked it dark.

But that noon was different. It was overwhelming. I was feeling things I couldn't comprehend. It was raining, and the sound of pouring rain pierced through the shut windows anyway. Quiet was far from reality.

A pencil snuck between my teeth, I pushed the window open, and struggled to anchor it. Then, I moved the table to where the window was. Drops of rain splattered onto the desk, and onto my face. I sat staring at the downpour with not a thought in mind. Before long, letters became words; words turned into phrases; and phrases, into verses. After a drought of eight weeks, poetry had come back to me that day, and my joy knew no bounds. Just then, the dark clouds took leave, leaving in their place white puffs of clouds. The rain stopped pouring, and the Sun took its place on the beautiful blue canvas again. This sudden change of scenery left me feeling light-headed. I grabbed another sheet from the printer, and scribbled all that I felt.

I was still writing, stealing occasional glances at the white clouds, when I heard a faint melody come to life. My eyes searched for the source, and before long, they were held captive by a silhouette. A silhouette of a man behind the window across the street. Our windows faced each other. It seemed as though he was looking at me as he played. I shivered.

My ears pricked for more details on the scarce notes that made their way to me. It sounded like *Lag Ja Gale*; a song that my mother hummed to me as a child, when she put me to sleep. A song that always made me wish I had had a love that could help me devour the melody the way it was meant to be devoured. I sat with my eyes closed, barely breathing.

Hours had passed before I reluctantly turned the lights off. Like they were connected to a single source, the lights in his room went off too. His windows closed as mine did.

I felt then, like I had made a friend. A familiar stranger.

It had all begun then.

We never spoke.

We never met.

But every evening, we sat by our windows facing each other, doing what we most loved doing. I scribbled poems on sheets, and he played one soul-stirring symphony after another!

Days went, and I couldn't get over the feeling that, perhaps, he was playing the songs for me. Like I wrote whatever I wrote, for him.

It was hard to tear my eyes from the window when he played. I ached to see him. But what if he vanished, when I went looking for him? What if tomorrow never came, and today was all I had of us? So, I stayed; writing poetry after poetry on this inexplicable feeling that surpassed love.

One evening, I kept the window closed, afraid of my unwarranted attachment to this silhouette. I found myself doubting if it had all been real. I sat biting my nails, struggling to make up my mind on breaking free of the habit I had so easily made. I had not gotten very far with it when I heard a shrill, painfully beautiful symphony. The notes beckoned to me, and I pushed the window open at once. The song came to an abrupt stop. He waited till I sat up straight, picked up my pencil and my sheet. Only when I was fully ready did he start playing again.

This time, it was not as agonizing. If I weren't thinking too much, it was a joyful pile of notes. I didn't know what to make of it except that this was a routine that was becoming indispensable.

The neighbours often spoke of a young man who lived across the street, all by himself. He never came out. Never spoke to his neighbours. He taught music to children.

I was certain that this man with the violin and that man with the reputation of a loner, were no different. What was his name? What kind of a person was he? What else did he do? Did he share the same absurdly intense feelings that I do? I knew nothing of him, and yet, the heart grew bigger each day.

Months passed, but he never stepped up. He never came to visit, nor did I go. Maybe, this was nothing more than an exchange of art. So, I devoured the time we spent together like any moment could be the last.

NOW

Reminiscing about the events of the past months, I pause writing. I look at him, with questions flooding my mind. He too has stopped playing.

If we were to talk, what would we talk about? Would we talk at all? We were nothing more than two art lovers who had learnt to better express their art forms, thanks to their routine.

If I were to lie to myself, this is exactly what I would tell. But we are more than that. I might be in love with him. At 29, I think I am old enough to differentiate between feelings of impulse, and those deeply rooted. If I were to think for him, I would tell you he is in love too. But I can't think for him.

What next? Are we to sit in front of our windows, forever longing for each other? Forever speaking through silence? I know better than to dream of a forever. I am happy with whatever persists. But I do not like stagnation. It's stifling.

Why hasn't he made an effort to meet me? Why won't I take the first stride? Is there another Universe perhaps, where we are not two, but one?

Take me there,
Where it's only you and I.
Take me there,
Where Earth meets the sky.
Take me there,
Where fish live in the sands.
Take me there,
Where stars glide into my hands.
Take me there,
Where we are alone, together.
Take me there,
Where, to each other, we'll surrender…

I am still writing, when I feel a tingling sensation within my heart. It feels like drops of rain on a parched land. My chest aches as the tingling spreads through my body, consuming every cell.

I feel light, as if I were a ball of cotton floating in the atmosphere. I can't help but think that my soul is departing at this exact moment. Must I worry? I can't seem to. Things around me start to feel light. The pencil I held has disappeared into nothingness. Everything looks hazy and blurry. Was this a dream, after all? Am I going to wake up and find out I have been dreaming all this while? I struggle to keep his silhouette in sight, when I hear a crumbling noise.

The dream's crumbling?

There's blinding light all around. Like, the tingling in my body has also consumed everything around me. There are shades of blue and pink anywhere I look.

Purple. Everything looks purple. The wall in front of me, which is a blinding purple with specks of white…or gold, is breaking. It crumbles into pieces. The window melts away. I do not understand what's going on.

Before I know it, my desk is on the edge of the ground. I peer down to look at the road beneath. But all I see is a void. I throw a glance at his window, and find the same empty nothingness in its place. The wall to his room too has crumbled. He is sitting on a chair, peering down the desk. His violin sits on his lap.

Everything is engulfed by a blanket of purple, it seems. Only he and I are left untouched; and our chairs, and his violin. The purple sky, if it is the sky at all, is starlit. I stay rooted to my chair. Any moment now, the dream will collapse.

Minutes later, everything is still intact. He has stopped staring at his desk, and is looking at me. Doesn't it scare him? I wonder.

"It does!", I hear a voice respond. I freeze. Is that him?

Confused, I ask again, "Doesn't this scare you?".

"It does. But it does not scare me as much as your idea of me.", he says.

It's him all right.

"What idea?", I ask defiantly.

"Your idea of the person I am. We are humans. We form ideas of each other, all the time. I am afraid of yours. I am afraid of your reaction to reality when you are brought to face it. I am afraid of the moment when you will realize that the past months have been nothing more than an exchange of a desire for art!", he says feebly.

I counter him. I negate him. I tell him I am sure of the gushing feelings. His stiff shoulders relax. He seems relieved; like I have told him just what he wanted to hear.

"Aren't you afraid of *my* idea of you?", he asks.

Now that I think of it, I may be a little afraid. But there's only so much I can do about his thoughts of me.

"Not really. I wouldn't worry about what is not in my control.", I tell him.

"Can you read me the verses you wrote for me? The first one? I have ached to hear them, for a long time now.", he says.

I look down on the sheets of paper on the table. My lips quiver, and my voice refuses to leave my throat. I had never thought of reading one of these to him. I had never thought the day would come.

I find myself a hypocrite. What was it that I was complaining of earlier? About wanting a flow? I had not thought even as far as reading my verses to him. Maybe I was happy where I had been; I had complained, because that's what humans do?

There is no going back now. I accede to his request.

"Bring me your heart,
Broken irrevocably.
I love broken things,
They lure me.
They crave to be loved,
And I crave to love.
So, let me heal
that heart of yours,
for that is how,
I will heal."

When I am done, he picks his bow without a word, and starts playing his violin. For the first time, the notes come to me in harmony…every note filling my swelling heart. I ache to get up from my chair, and walk to him. I ache for a million things all at once. He is still playing with his eyes tightly shut, when I see swirls of purple. I see golden guiding stars.

In no time, a path has been drawn on the colourful canvas in front of me. A path hanging mid-air.

Without a second thought, I place a foot on the path. It does not sink; I do not fall. I look ahead and see it leading to him. I run.

When there are only a few strides left, I have to drag my feet, for they won't move. For my eyes have seen him. They have seen not his silhouette, but him. In his being. I know I am not breathing; I know I am still alive.

Is it possible that when an organ fails, another steps up in its place? It seems to me like, in this moment, my eyes are breathing, taking in his face with every step I walk towards him. My palms are feeling hot *and* cold. Blood is rushing through my veins, *and* at the same time, draining. My limbs are jittery, *and yet* so sure. I witness my body breaking every scientific rule ever.

As he draws his string for the last note, I too take my last step towards him. When he opens his eyes, I am standing in front of him, my own eyes shut. I can't look at him, not yet.

I have come this far, but he has not left his chair. I ache for him to take just one step towards me, to tell me we are both swirling in this chaotic mess of feelings together. I wait for him to speak. But he does not. I wait for him to come to me. Minutes become hours, but I sense no movement.

My breaking heart threatens to stop beating, and I force my eyes open. The stars make me hazy, and I can no longer hold my ground. I look at him still at his desk; still holding his violin.

Without a word, I begin to walk back to my room. I turn for one last glance at his face. I shudder at the look in his eyes.

"I told you I am afraid of your reaction to reality. I did not realize you would refuse to even see it.", he says.

I don't understand a word of it. I begin running towards my chair. He starts playing the violin. I hear an agonizing melody chase me. I run faster.

He won't stop playing. My heart won't stop breaking.

My alarm startles me, and I wake up tired. I realize I have slept on my desk on a crumpled sheet of paper. The agonizing melody still rings in my ears, bringing back all that transpired. I can't tell if it was real. The notes tug at my heart, and I can't shake them off. I look at his window, it's shut. There's no trace of purple anywhere today. The walls are intact and the stars are gone. Could it have really been a dream?

I struggle to get past the day, waiting anxiously for the evening to come. When it does come, I am standing by the door, staring at it. Readjusting my bag for the 19th time, I think of things to say. The events of yesterday might have been a dream. But what if they were real? What if he remembers all of it, like I do?

"I told you I am afraid of your reaction to reality. I did not realize you'd refuse to even see it.", he had said.

So, I stand at his door, to make sure I see the reality he intended for me to see. I ring the bell and wait. Minutes pass before the door swings open.

I see him.

He looks just like he did yesterday. Pursed lips that curved into a smile; kind eyes that crinkle as he smiles. He continues to sit, reading me in amusement.

"You are here to see the reality?" he asks.

I stare at him blankly, astounded by the fact that it all did happen. We did see each other last night then. He did say what I thought he did.

"Any moment now?", he smiles.

The ugly turn that yesterday's events took fills my mind. He had refused to take that one step. Why?

I struggle to speak.

Leaving me at the door, he goes inside humming the agonizing melody he had played yesterday. I can't hear it over his whirring wheelchair's motor.

"Any moment now?", he repeats.

I finally see it.

12

Bubbles

A little boy was watching his mother watering the plants in their garden, when round glass-like nothings flew in the air above him. They were big and small. Where were they coming from? Was it magic? He was sure it was!

"What's that, mother?", He squealed in amusement.

Never had he seen them before.

"Those are called bubbles!", she said.

"I want bubbles, mother!", he shrieked, and ran to where they were flying.

When he got closer, he saw that they were delicate. So, slowing his breath, he tried catching a bubble, barely touching it.

But it popped.

He gasped and looked at his mother who was smiling.

"Try again.", she said.

The boy tried catching a different bubble, this time holding his breath.

Again, it popped.

He whispered endearingly to the bubble he was after.

"You will be okay. Just come to me!", he said.

But the bubbles kept popping.

Chasing them, he had walked quite a distance away from where he had sat. He was desperate to keep a bubble for himself. He began clapping furiously, and winced every time his hands met. Little did he realise that he was hurting himself trying to catch something that never could be his.

After what seemed like hours to the boy, he sat down sobbing. His mother sat next to him and pressed his pink hands.

"What you want, you don't always need. Look at your hands, my little baby. This is what it will do to you. You see. Life will give you beautiful things that will find its way to you, and stay. Without you having to hurt yourself like this!", she told him.

Just then, a bright yellow butterfly flew up to him out of nowhere, and sat on his hand. He shrieked in excitement as it fluttered its wings.

"Didn't I tell you?", his mother smiled.

13

A Distressed Little Soul

THE STORYTELLER

I must call Avih, for it's time for her to get going.

She is going to put up a fight yet again. But this time, I am afraid I can't let her have her way. They have taken it too far, the twain.

You know how they say that, you grind in the initial days, so you can sit back and relax later on? It's a lie. I still have an overflowing list of things that I must look after.

They are a handful, my children.

But I shouldn't complain; for it's only when they visit home that I have to don the hat of a supervisor…a parent…a friend. When they go out on their own to live a life of their choice, I have not a thing to do. They seldom ask for my intervention *there*. So, every time they cause a ruckus while visiting, I simply laugh it off.

I call out to Avih from where I am. No response. I am convinced she has heard me. But she refuses to acknowledge my call. I will walk to where she is, then.

She has come home for a break, before she is off for her next performance.

The stage is her only solace, she tells me.

I think that's the case for all the little ones in our family. I have been weaving stories for eons now. Naturally, the kids grew up to be ardent story lovers themselves;

all of them capable of holding lengthy conversations on why I wrote a certain character in a certain way. They have blamed me for some storylines and praised me for some; but there's not a story till date that they have not loved.

One day, when I was mulling over how to get started with life, the children walked to me and told me they were ready to take my work far and wide. They did not want the stories to remain confined to our home, serving no purpose. All of the Universe must know of my love for storytelling, they insisted.

They decided they would choose from the plethora of roles from my archive, go out there themselves and portray all the characters I have penned; just as I had hoped they would do.

Go, they did, and perform; and they did justice to every role they donned.

But things are slowly starting to change. This will only be the first of many changes to come, if I do not reprimand the ones at fault: Avih and Viti.

They have not been getting along lately. I seldom know when they come and go. This time when Avih goes back, I have to convince her to accept, for once, to play the part I want her to. Having to forfeit the liberty to choose the role in one play, is not asking for too much, is it? If I do not do it now, the other children will come to know of the incident and follow suit.

I put my heart and soul into creating each play. I can't allow their tiff to cause havoc.

Viti is out fulfilling her role as Rekha. She is as lost and miserable as Avih is.

VITI AS REKHA

The clock has struck two, and Rekha is struggling to stay awake. She has washed the dishes, tidied the kitchen, watered each one of her twelve plants, and even pulled off a few yoga postures better than she had yesterday. Staring at the wall in front, she is chopping vegetables. Her last chore for the day. She chops with a monotony one would never have witnessed before, wearing an expression of a veteran murderer. One can't blame her, for a human being needs sleep to function. And lately, she has barely had any. She hasn't slept for nights.

'Why, she could take a nap during the day, can't she?' One might ask. And she would tell them a story of how on the second day of her battle with sleep, she had willingly lost and taken a long nap. Unfortunately, the duration of her nap had coincided with the incessant ringing of the calling bell. When she had opened the door, crease marks on her cheeks and dried drool patches on her chin had brought out laughter from her guests: her parents in-law. They were in town for a day and thought they would drop by for a quick visit, they told her. She wondered if the committee of elders had even the slightest idea of how no one in the age group of 20-40 ever looked forward to quick, unannounced visits.

"Did you have trouble sleeping last night?", her mother-in-law had asked.

"No, no. The weather today got me sleeping again…", Rekha had laughed.

Her in-laws had quietly exchanged glances.

Glances that Rekha translated to be, "She does not even go to work like our Manoj does. I wonder what makes her so sleepy!".

They had left after coffee, without commenting further on the incident. The whole family had come to know of it.

Cringing at the memory of the day, she decides she would scream the truth into their ears if they visited again.

"I have not slept for nights because of your son!", she would shout.

With the last chore for the day done, she walks into their bedroom thinking of her in-laws' possible discussions on her being home.

"It is not like I want to stay home all day anyway. I must be the one complaining about my being home.", she says out loud.

Sitting on her side of the bed, her legs sprawled to occupy every bit of her space, she looks around the room. It's powder blue in colour. This was the shade of Manoj's shirt when they had first met. She had set this room up from scratch. Not only this room. The whole house.

A year ago, when they had moved into this house after their wedding, Manoj had left the interior styling to her choice.

“It’s only fair that you decide how the house looks. Because you are going to be the one that spends more time here!”, he had said.

As harmless as his intention was, she had felt hurt. But she had kept quiet. Turning her face away from Manoj and his statement, she had chosen to focus instead, on the project in hand. She had begun work immediately. She had hand-drawn the look she envisioned for the house, and made a list of the furniture pieces they would need. She knew a lot, if not all, about the colours and aesthetics that went into making a nook look artistic. It came to her naturally.

That was also why she was a great photographer.

At 16, when she had first realized her love for photography, she decided to make a career out of it. With hardly a year left to finish her schooling, she started to throw hints to her parents on her interest in pursuing Visual Communication in college. They were quick to catch it, and quicker to deny it.

Having been the daughter of an austere household for years, she was not new to the art of negotiation. Except, negotiation worked differently in their house. As loud and argumentative as she was, the only way she knew to get her parents’ approval for one thing, was to tell them she would forfeit something else she had that they were not keen on. And if she had to let go of something she liked, she would ask for something else in bargain. Little did she realize then that she did not have to give up on anything, at all, if she really wanted it.

When she turned 18, before she applied to universities, her father spoke to her again. He wanted to ensure she was clear on the terms and conditions that came with the permission to pursue the course which every one of their relatives had deemed useless. 1. She would go to a women's college. 2. He would drop her at college. 3. He would pick her up. Every day.

Considering the setting of their household, she was not keen on entering love relationships anyway. She dreaded the efforts it would demand of her. In that sense, she found it to be a good bargain.

Every morning, her father would give her a ride to the college on his bike, all the while complaining about how the meaning of education had changed over the years.

"Back in our days, we pursued courses we were sure would fetch us a job. We studied subjects that would help us and the society in some way or the other. Pointless courses, these days!", he would mumble.

She would remind him of his obsession with films and shows. She would tell him that he would have none, if there were no photography-loving humans.

And in the evening, standing amidst a crowd of young men waiting for their girlfriends, would be her father judging the 'jobless boys' as he liked to call them. All the way back home, they would bicker about 'her generation'.

She did great in college and bagged a job as an assistant to a renowned photographer. She had a month's time before she reported to her job. But that time had been enough for her parents to find her a groom. She had no say, unsurprisingly.

"Be grateful we have found you a groom who does not live with his parents. With your stubborn, argumentative nature, you would have had trouble.", they had told her.

They had a way with words, and she had been swayed enough by them to be grateful for their careful consideration.

Sighing at the memory of her naivete, she rolls around the bed and lets out another yawn. Being in the bedroom won't help her stay awake. So, she walks to the kitchen and pours herself a cup of coffee which is barely warm. A year ago, if she had been told she wouldn't mind drinking coffee that was not ice cold, but was not piping hot either, she would have laughed at them. *Who would ever drink coffee like that?*

Sipping on the drink that's as lifeless as she is, she goes into the 'extra room' as the couple calls it. Her cosy haven. She had set it up for all things work and hobbies, and painted the walls a calming aqua blue. She looks at the 'wall of frame' - a name she still prides herself over.

Dotted with frames of pictures she had captured during her days as a student, the wall is the only place in this entire house that reminds her of her wilting dreams. She was an aspiring photographer then; she is an aspiring photographer today. She would be an aspiring photographer forever.

Her thoughts race back to the day the couple had travelled together for the first time after their betrothal. Sitting in the car after their date, they had spent a long time talking. Manoj, who was six years older than her, was a soft-spoken man and a great listener. She had taken an instant liking to him, and his calm demeanour. During the course of their conversation, she had told him of her dreams to become the best photographer in the city.

"I had even landed a job as an assistant photographer which I can't go to now. It's okay, I am sure I can find another job soon! I can't wait to put my camera to good use!", she had said.

Laughing at her as he stroked her cheek, he had replied, "Of course. You can be our personal photographer. We can click a million pictures together."

Rekha had blushed, for that was the first time he had touched her face. When the initial daze passed, her heart sank at his statement. Gritting her teeth, she thought of a million things she could tell him to make him understand she was serious about her dream. In the end, she had not said anything at all. Neither had he broached the subject again. Not then; not after their wedding.

She had convinced herself that the only reason she was not at work already was because she was busy setting up the house. Once she was done with it, she would head right out.

But, months ago, when she had finished 'project home', she could not bring up the subject of photography. There was barely any room in their conversations for a discussion on work and career. Manoj spoke to her of kids in a tense that scared her; like they would knock at the door any moment, and ask the couple to be their parents. She saw her dreams fade.

He was a nice person, there was no denying *that*. But so was she.

The problems in her life never rose because someone was not being nice. They came because of her own inability to be *anything* but nice to *anyone* at all, at *any hour* of the day. She did everything to please everyone she was associated with. Then she began to dislike them for failing to understand something she *could* not, and *did* not convey. Oh, how many people she had lost because they couldn't read between the lines. She was afraid the same fate would befall her relationship with her husband. She did not like to even think of it. If only she could voice her thoughts. It was not like she had none, she had plenty all the time. So many, simultaneously.

Dragging the bean bag to face the window, she sits down with her half empty cup of coffee. Her phone chimes.

It's a text message from her younger sister asking her if she spoke to Manoj about their problem. Rekha does not want to reply to the message, for she has not yet spoken to Manoj. It would only make her sister mad. For the last few days, she has messaged Rekha every morning to check if she had had a good night's sleep, and if she had had 'the talk' with Manoj. And, every morning, Rekha had replied with a meek 'No :(', to both her questions. It irks her to say so again, today.

Her sister didn't understand her struggle. She never would. She was born mute, and was a great deal better at getting things done. She could not argue or shout like Rekha was always seen doing; but she had nods and gestures that were firmer than her elder sister's string of words. With her, it was either a strong yes or a strong no. There was never a moment of doubt.

Growing up, there were days when Rekha wished she had been born mute instead. The business with words confused her. Their meaning depended on too many factors, and could be perceived any way by the audience. That scared her. So, she put great efforts into sounding just about right and balanced in every conversation she ever had. Having been born as someone with the ability to talk, she felt handicapped.

Rekha is destined for greater things, but look at her struggle.

It's evident that Viti needs Avih. And Avih, Viti.

I am sure you too would agree with me.

Oh.

...

.....

Apologies.

I hope you're not having trouble connecting the rather vague dots. I would not blame you, for there's no reason for you to be aware of the happenings of our realm.

If I am telling you a story, I might as well give you all the details you need, to be able to fully understand it.

Like I stated earlier, I am the creator of stories and plays. I create characters and give them a role to fulfil in the play that's referred to as life, in your world.

I am the author of the story that Rekha is living; it's donned by Viti. The story that you are living now, I wrote that too. That you're reading this even as we speak, all part of the play. Every story that you see around you, I know by heart.

To spell it out for you, I am God.

When I first created the story-bearers, the souls, I cleaved them into two even as I birthed them. Because I knew that they would have to, sooner or later, travel far and wide all by themselves. The world is a frightening place to be, if one's alone. It won't do to send them afar and leave them feeling homesick, only for them to want to abandon their role midway and come back home.

So, I sent them together. In pairs. Always.

It did not matter whether they set out on the journey at the same time or not; as did not the fact that they either remained acquainted for life, or crossed paths only once in a birth. Whatever their respective stories demanded.

But they had to be part of each other's story. They had to know so.

Because, although they were two, they were one. Like Avih and Viti.

Three lives ago, Avih and Viti got themselves into a rather ugly mess.

They were engaged in playful banter when they were home. They could go separate ways and lead their lives all by themselves without one another, they told me. They claimed that it wasn't as big a deal as I made it seem. It went too far, and they decided they must see for themselves what happens. Before I knew it, the twain had gone against the norm and picked stories where they had nothing to do with each other. Stories where one did not know of the other's existence.

They were apprehensive and counting on each other to back off. But neither did. So, they went to the world and lived their own distressed lives, the distressed little soul.

When she came back after her first life without Viti, a pale-faced Avih had not said a word. She had quietly gone around our home looking for Viti. She did not find her, for Viti had still been out fulfilling her role. Restless and anxious, Avih had chosen another story, another life, where Viti had no part to play. She went on to live yet another life in misery. She did not want to be the weakling who gave in.

Neither did Viti, when she returned after leading a miserable life herself. They were two peas of the same pod, after all. Two halves of the same soul.

As a result, the twain has each led three lives without one another. Why, they have not seen each other in ages. What started off as harmless fun has now caused chaos in lives, theirs and the humans'.

Because, while their stories are not dependent on each other, the story-bearers, Avih and Viti, are. While the characters they played did not have much to do with each other, Avih and Viti did. Their being apart was unbearable to them, and their distress oozed into the stories of the characters they played. The aches and desires of the story-bearers tampered with the very story.

A man spent his life pining for his soulmate, his lover, but found none till his end, although she was right there. Because Avih refused to acknowledge anyone but Viti as his soulmate.

A woman ached for the comfort of a sister she never had, for Viti refused to feel as strongly for the brother for whom she was the destined soul sister.

Yet another young man looked at every passer-by with hope, only to watch them go on without a second glance. He was sure one of them was going to change his life for good, but he could not recognize them. Avih chose not to.

Viti, having already failed two humans, is now in the middle of her third life without Avih. She has a long way to go as Rekha - a confused misfit in her world.

Avih and Viti have suffered; So have my characters, without an encounter with their twin flames. They have let down humans, so many. I can't allow them to go on like this, forever. Because, I have heard from the neighbouring Universe about the unfortunate event of souls leaving their human containers owing to unbearable grief. Those are some badly written stories for the souls, if you ask me. It's an unacceptable fallacy. The mishaps there scare me. For we have no Man-Tortoise Dyads in *our* Universe, to console homesick souls abandoning characters midway.

Which is why, it is up to me to lead them back to one another. At once.

Which is also why I have had to tamper with a pre-written story; to create room for Avih, in Viti's life.

VITI AS REKHA

Rekha massages her temples and tries to think of the last time she had a good night's sleep. She counts on her fingers. It has been 10 days. That means 'The talk' with Manoj is due by 10 days as of today. She runs her tongue over her teeth in disgust. The coffee has suddenly turned unbearably bitter. Or, it's the bile. She pours the rest of the coffee down the kitchen drain.

Leaning by the counter, she tells herself that the power to realize her dreams reside in her hands. She had been their school's head-girl, after all. Younger students had been terrified of rousing her anger. She had had friends who loved her company. She had delivered so many speeches on stage, each earning a thunderous applause from the audience.

They would not believe her, if she called one of them now, and told them she had trouble speaking up. They would guffaw, thinking it was yet another joke of hers. She is smiling to herself, when something strikes her. She decides she must prepare a similar speech for Manoj, penning down all that needs to be said. She would hand it over to him when he came home in the evening. And then, she would have a good night's sleep.

She walks back to the study with renewed energy, and sits at her desk. The doorbell rings. Could it be her in-laws again?

"Not making a fool of myself this time around", she tells herself. Determined to not leave a long gap between the ringing and her answering the door, she runs maniacally. This time, her in-laws would be forced to think that she is the briskest person they have ever known.

When she opens the door struggling to swallow her breathless panting, she is surprised to find her aunt instead. Her father's younger sister who lives down the road, but thankfully never troubled herself enough to come visit the couple, has come home all of a sudden. Rekha lets a gasp escape, bringing a smile from her aunt.

An hour later, after talking about things that are of no importance to either of the two women, her aunt clears her throat.

"I came here to ask a favour.", she finally says.

Rekha narrows her eyes in confusion and nods.

"It's my daughter, Nisha.", she says.

"What happened to her Athhai*? Is she okay?", Rekha panics.

"She is okay. Why wouldn't she be? She has had everything go her way, after all. It's us who are not okay. Your Mama** and I.", she sighs exasperatedly.

Her thoughts run in all directions before her aunt begins her monologue. Rekha, knowing she has no part to play in this, leans back and listens.

---

* Father's Sister/Aunt

** Aunt's husband

"She is three years elder to you and is still unmarried, you know. She throws tantrums like a child every time we broach the subject to her. She is drawing and stitching clothes all the time. In the mornings, she goes to the boutique to work for that designer woman who claims to be the best in the state. She is going to be the reason for Nisha's downfall, I tell you! When she comes back home in the evening, she goes straight into her room, to her desk covered in chalk dust. She says she wants to set up a boutique, and that she won't think of marriage till she does. This girl! All these months your Mama and I ignored her claims thinking she was just confused. We thought she would realize that all her talks about financial independence mean nothing. As long as she is under our roof, we would be able to make her see our point, we thought. But last week, she threw yet another boulder on our shoulders. She wants to go to the USA to pursue a master's degree in designing… the talk about dreams, it sickens me. Why! Did I not have dreams? Didn't your amma have dreams of her own? We understood our priority and chose what was right for everyone. This girl…she talks about being in a foreign country all by herself for two years. Will anybody want to marry someone who is living so far away from parental supervision? You tell me!", she cries, throwing her hands in the air.

Rekha, confused by the sudden invitation to speak, clears her throat and leans forward, when her aunt gets going again.

"I don't know what to say to her. You were such a sweet child. Your parents are blessed. From when you were a child, I have not seen your Appa or Amma come crying to me about your behaviour. "Just a loud chatter box…but she is a good girl", they would tell me. Seeing you, I wonder where I went wrong. I remember you were possessed by the ghost of a dream-chasing girl for a bit, running around with your toy camera. But you recovered. You saw your parents' point, understood that all the talk about dreams didn't make sense, and got married like a good girl, didn't you? Your mother was worried you would start talking about career after marriage. But look at you…you give them no reason to worry. I wish Nisha would learn from you! Married or unmarried, girls your age need to stop talking about selfish dreams. Talk to Nisha, for me, will you? You two have always been good friends. Your Athhai has no other hope. Please, kanna…", she finished, sighing.

What she does not notice in her own preoccupation is a blanched Rekha.

Her eyes are brimming with tears that won't fall. There's a growing lump in her throat that threatens to explode. She grits her teeth and runs to her study without a word. Safe inside the room, she sobs noiselessly. She grieves for her inability to speak. She grieves for her inability to put up a fight. She grieves for her dying dreams. She feels alone. She feels she is all by herself in this vast world. Like her guardian angel took the wrong flight down to their world, leaving her to fend for herself.

Afraid her aunt might come in search of her, she wipes her face dry, clears her throat and concentrates on breathing steadily. Ashamed of herself, she walks back to the living room to find her aunt still sitting with her head in her hands.

"I will talk to her, Athhai!" Rekha tells her, attempting to sound assuring.

After showering her with heaps of praises and thanks, Athhai walks out of the door leaving Rekha alone to her thoughts.

She walks straight to their bedroom, and looks at the bed. She winces. She is exhausted. Her first step towards taking control over her life again, she decides, would be to win back her side of the bed. To win back her sleep.

Few days into their marriage, Manoj had realized he was not able to spend much time with Rekha owing to his night-shift at work. He had promised her that he would move to a regular shift in a year.

10 days ago, he had reported to his day job at a new workplace, and stuck to his end of the promise.

"This is my anniversary gift to you!", he had smiled at her.

It all started that night when it was time to sleep. The couple got into bed, and Manoj dozed off. Hours later, Rekha was still staring into the dark, balancing herself in one corner of the bed. Manoj tossed and rolled and sprawled all over the bed, leaving no place for her. When dawn broke, she went to the living room and slept on the couch. She must tell him he is a bad sleeper, she decided before she fell asleep.

Come morning, when he had woken her up, she had sheepishly told him she had snuck out for a midnight snack and fallen asleep there. She cursed herself for lying thus. But that was not new to her.

That night, the illegal occupation of her side of the bed recurred. The following noon was when her in-laws had visited. When he had come home that evening, Manoj had had the audacity to laugh at her.

"Heard from Amma that you slept the whole day away, sleepy sloth!", he said.

Still unable to confront him on a matter so trivial, she spent her energy thinking of ways to keep her side of the bed for herself.

Till 10 days ago, Manoj had always slept in his after-shift hours, even on weekends. He did not like messing up his sleep cycle. Now he was messing with Rekha's.

When it was time to sleep that third night, she had brought bolsters from the living room, and laid them in between them.

"I want to put my legs over something as I sleep", she grinned.

Laughing at her, he had thrown them away and said, "What am I here for?".

Another sleepless night followed, and she was exhausted. It was not her trespassing husband who angered her. It was herself, yet again. She spent the day coming up with a plan to claim her side of the bed without waking Manoj. But come night, her plans failed again. None could defeat the usurper, as she had begun to think of him.

On the 6th night, when he almost pushed her off the bed, she reached for his arm and pinched him. He had yelped and woken up for a moment, before he went back to sleep on his side of the bed. She pinched her way through the night. When morning came, she could not face him. The guilt ate her, and she ended up grating three bags of carrots to make him his favourite carrot halwa*. He had been pleasantly surprised and promised her a late-night movie date.

10 nights have passed thus, and the 11th is around the corner. There's no time to prepare a speech. She decides to tell him everything as it is. She would talk

* Pudding

to him about her side of the bed. She would tell him how she has suffered without sleep. About how he tosses and pushes and greedily occupies her side of the bed too.

If she is talking about this, she might as well talk to him about her career. She could talk to him about waiting for a few years before they became parents. She would suggest getting a maid, so she could focus more on developing her skills as a photographer. She would talk to him against watching movies late in the night, for the storyline went over her head. She would ask him to wash his plates after he had eaten off them, so it would become easier for her. She could tell him how she enjoyed shopping on her own. She would convince him that buses and autos were not as dangerous as he made them seem. She should talk to him about everything trivial and significant that she had refrained from telling him, she decides! What harm would come? He would *understand* the message, if she only *conveyed* the message. She must not let her inability to tell him then and there how she felt, result in her growing hatred towards him.

Having decided on the course of action, she sits down on the bed and sends a message to Nisha.

"Married or unmarried, don't give up on your dreams. They can wait, yes, owing to changing priorities. But they are not meant to be forgotten. They are our only chance at carving an identity for ourselves!".

In response, she is flooded with hearts of every colour that take up her whole screen. Smiling, she wishes she could respect herself too, the way her cousin respected herself.

I don't feel good about tampering with the story. But it's my last resort to help Avih and Viti resolve their juvenile conflict. Besides, it won't be long before the other children ask to be sent down separate paths, should they come to know of Avih and Viti's solo adventures. I ought to fix this before chaos stretches its arms and decides to settle here for good.

I see Avih gazing at the nothingness that surrounds her.

"It's time for you to go!", I say.

"But I only just got here!", she snaps.

"Still hung on the grumpy character we played a while ago, are we?"

She says nothing.

"Alright, it's time for you to go. This time, you will be playing a character I favour. I have picked it especially for you, and it demands you start now.", I say.

"But, why? Everyone else gets to pick their stories. Why don't I? What's the fun in playing a role I am not keen on?", she asks, hurt.

"Because, listen. Owing to various reasons, I had to tamper with a pre-written story. I have had to make changes to it. Because, the story, and the story-bearer were on the brink of disintegration, and needed saving. All that's left is for you to play your role, and have the story completed as has been rewritten.", I try to sound stern.

Avih stares at me struggling to comprehend whatever I told her.

"What's the story?", she asks.

"There's this girl…who is lost. She is fumbling her way through life, and is about to put herself in a spot. She may be a weakling now…but you will be the reason she flies high. You will be the reason she stands up tall, and finally sets things right.", I say.

"But can't she do it herself?"

"Of course, she could have done it on her own too… she is definitely not incapable. But not in this life, is all. Not in this story. This is how her story plays out, this time. And it's okay that she needs you…", I pull Avih closer to me.

"It seems to me like you've already made up your mind. Can I, at least, see?"

Smiling at her, I sit down to witness Rekha's story unfold. Avih gasps.

VITI AS REKHA

It's night again, and the clock has struck 11. Manoj and Rekha climb into the bed. Her heart won't stop beating and she has trouble breathing. She looks at him and she smiles. She loves the man, she realizes. But she would love him a lot more, when she could be herself. Making up her mind, she turns his face towards hers, and tells him she wants to talk to him.

He immediately tosses his phone to his side, and looks at her.

"I think...I think we need to get a bigger bed. A King-sized bed perhaps?", she manages to say.

Before she has time to be relieved at how cleverly she has been able to resolve the problem, she gasps in astonishment.

Because Manoj is smiling. He is beaming. His face is lit with ecstasy like she has never seen before. His heart is beating fast, and he gazes at her lovingly. She balls her right hand that's on his chest, into a fist, as her own heart sinks deeper with every passing moment.

Tears cloud her eyes when he gently places his hand on her stomach, caresses it, and nods his head questioningly. Not knowing what else to say, she nods in turn and allows him to pull her into a crushing hug. She lets her tears drop onto his shoulder, when she tastes bile in her mouth.

Rushing to the wash basin, she vomits. And that only goes on to aid her lie.

She sees her dreams going down the drain of her basin. She can't do anything to stop them. Then, she feels a hand patting her back. Manoj is holding her head gently, and whispering calming words. She washes her mouth, desperate to cleanse it off of everything she has ever said against her wish.

Going back to the bed, she pulls him towards her and makes love to him.

She has a lie that needs to be made true, after all.

THE STORYTELLER

I sent Avih off on her journey to Earth again. She was an eager mess when she left; for it is in this life that she will be the closest to Viti.

As for me, I sit back and watch Avih and Viti make their way towards each other. It's time for their mother-daughter play to unfold.

14

Heart in School

Years ago, there once lived a little boy called Heart. He was a happy child. Till he had to learn. Learn.

He soon joined a school called Life. Teaching began right after!

Many lessons, many teachers. Some easy, some difficult. Some lessons nearly sucked the life out of him. They made him wince when he thought of them. Some made him wish he never woke up. He did not want to go to school. He simply did not.

Lessons after lessons continued. Teachers so many: Love and Lust, Impatience and Patience, Loss, Hope, Envy, Trust... too many to count. Too many to take in.

There were days he wanted to flee from the school, the urge so strong. But, where would he go? He could not.

He would close his eyes, hoping for the lesson to be done when he opened his eyes again. But, no! The teacher would still be there, refusing to leave till the point was made.

He complained, he cried. Because, no matter how hard he tried, he could never be prepared for the lessons. They always struck him hard, when they came. He was lagging behind. With all the lessons piling up, nearly crushing him beneath them, he experienced to the fullest extent, the pain he was put through.

He was so close to giving up. The only thing that stopped Heart from doing so, was the light at the end of the tunnel that all of his teachers spoke of. Beyond that was a world where there was no pain. Beyond that was a world where there were no worries. He wanted to see that.

Gritting his teeth, he gave in to the school's way of taking him to the light.

He gave up clinging on to the pain the lessons put him through. Little could he seek revenge.

He did not close his eyes when lessons stung. He did not complain. He took it all in, whatever was taught, barely wincing. He understood, he agreed. They made sense. And he made peace.

Soon, he found himself smiling every time a new teacher walked in. He craved to know what form the lessons would take. He looked forward to the beauty of it. He no longer resisted them.

One day, all of his teachers gathered around him and showed him the light that they spoke so highly of. It was shining from within him. With a smile on his face, Heart finally stepped out of the school, shining in all his glory.

15

Ghostly Enlightenment

RAMU AND HIS WISH

"Amma, someone threw a plate. I heard it. I am sure it's a ghost", a sleepy Ramu shook his mother's arm to wake her up.

It must have been half past 12; Ramu had been in a slumber till he had heard a plate crashing, or so he stated. When he opened his eyes, everything was still. His eyes sparkling with fervour, he convinced his mother to sit up and look around; maybe the ghost would be visible to her eyes. That way, he too would finally get to meet a ghost he thought, shivering within.

Everyone in his house had had a rendezvous with one ghost or the other. His elder brothers, the twins, had told their mother how they had seen a figure strangling her neck. Whenever they complained of there being a ghost nearby, Radhamma would sit up and lift the broomstick next to her, and call out loudly to the ghosts.

"Wait till I catch you and beat you to a pulp."

The ghosts that were supposedly scared of broomsticks and slippers, would scurry away. Ramu's father, who did not believe in ghosts, always brushed the stories away. But one midnight, a year ago, when he had gone out to the fields to relieve himself, he had been humbled. He had seen two figures wavering in the air in front of him, laughing loudly. He had been petrified till the ghosts politely flew away. And even afterwards, if truth be told.

Ramu had never once seen a ghost and he was convinced that this night was going to be the night. But

Radhamma simply pulled him close to her, and patted him to sleep.

'Why don't the ghosts ever meet me? If they don't meet me soon, even Vidhya would have met one! I really wish I could meet a ghost…' Ramu thought wincing, before he slipped back into his slumber.

GANEHALLI

The family lived in a village called Ganehalli, in a small house with tiled-roof. The residential area of the village was itself divided into clusters of houses, with patches of land in between left unoccupied. No one ever built standalone houses in the empty stretch, for the fear of their homes being home to the ever-wandering ghosts. Instead, they went on building their houses around one cluster or the other, careful not to let two clusters mix, for reasons unknown to anyone.

Decades later, some villagers dared to set up shops in between clusters, to attract maximum sales. After setting up a shop, they would build a house behind it, claiming they wanted to be able to serve the villagers who came to their shop round the clock. The houses multiplied, so as for it to become a mini cluster in itself. Naturally, those who owned shops began to be regarded as the leaders of their small village; what with their own clusters and their valour!

Ramachari was the first in their village to set up his own cluster, and the first to be crowned the Head, with no opposition at all! He was a jolly old man, after all. At least, he had been a jolly old man, for as long as he had been alive.

In that small village, Ramu's family led a mundane life; each day was the same as the previous, and the same as the next would be. His father Krishnappa, was the headmaster of their village's only school. A hefty man of forty years, despite not owning a cluster, he was still regarded as one of the many leaders of the village. To show him in a good light, Radhamma urged him to go to school earlier than required, so every parent that happened to stop by the school would see Krishnappa already present.

'What a punctual man!', she wanted them to say.

If they said so at all, nobody knows. But the schedule was strictly followed.

Radhamma woke up at five, and Krishnappa at six. She would cook breakfast for the family and have it ready in time for Krishnappa's consumption after his unbelievably quick bath. He was a slow eater, and his family was ever grateful for this trait of his. While he ate, Ramu's elder brothers would wake up, bathe, eat and get ready. Then, the three would leave for school.

With them gone, Radhamma would sit down by the doorstep to enjoy a few moments' peace before Ramu and Vidhya woke up. It was around the same time that Vani, Seeta and Kamali from the neighbouring houses came outside, one by one. Sitting by their respective doorsteps with all of their husbands off to work, the women would discuss the woes of their lives.

Oh, how the family would suffer, if they took off from their duties for even a day! They were indispensable! If only the kids and their husbands realized this.

"You're home all day, what do you know of a man's plight?", the husbands would ask, if they showed even mild signs of fatigue. At that moment, they would want to sit their husbands down and make them etch on a rock all that they, the wives did, as they dictated; lest they ask them the same question again – of plight and men!

But they never sat them down and never delivered the monologue that they had, so many times, rehearsed in their minds.

'Poor husbands! They don't cope with stress so well.', they would say, and cut them slack. Then they would compare themselves with women from other clusters with the many rumours they had come to hear, and later convince themselves that they were definitely better off.

It was an eternal cycle of blaming the husbands to vent their frustration, and then taking the blame back lest the other women judged their husbands. The point of this discussion, nobody arrived at.

RAMU AND VIDHYA

6-year-old Ramu never knew what to do with himself. His two elder brothers woke up early and went to school. He had to wait for another long year before he too could start going.

His little sister, Vidhya, was only a year younger than he was. How much he hated her, only he knew. Of course, she did. For even when she was a baby, Ramu would crawl over to her cradle and pinch the sleeping child, when no one was around. Leaving a wailing baby behind, a laughing Ramu would scurry.

Sometimes he did not like to even think that he did that to her. Because she never harmed him. It was his mother. Also, his father. *Their* mother. *Their* father. How they pampered Vidhya, calling her 'Kandha[*]'. Kandha was *his* name! Realizing that she was not the source of his problems, he would crawl over to the cradle and kiss her feet and palms apologetically. He was torn between the love and hate he had for her then. But as years passed, he obtained clarity on his feelings towards her. He hated her. She was a useless being, he often thought to himself.

But she did not think so of him.

She would clumsily walk behind him all the time, chanting "Anna[**]...anna".

---

* An endearing term used to address a younger person

** Elder brother

Ramu would get furious. How could he, a boy so big, play with a being so small! Why wouldn't she understand? He would flee from the house. Better to get roasted in the scorching sun than to be caught in the house with her.

Years had passed, but nothing changed in their relationship. Vidhya doted on Ramu; Ramu could not stand the sight of Vidhya.

"Why is she in this house?", Ramu asked his mother every day, without fail. "She is the Lakshmi* of this house!", Radhamma would reply, illogically. With Vidhya around, he could not have a moment's peace.

"Somanna and Nandanna have both gone to school. Why don't you play with me? It will be fun!", Vidhya would ask him every day, without fail. "I can never play with you. You're not a boy, and you're small!", Ramu would reply, illogically. Without him around, Vidhya did not know what to do with herself.

Radhamma, who had been the sole witness to Ramu's insecurity when Vidhya was born, decided to give him more time to cope with the fact that he was not the youngest in the house anymore. It had only been 5 years! Naive little Ramu would need a few more years' time.

How many tantrums he had thrown when he first realized that she was going to stay in this house forever.

* Goddess of wealth and fortune in Hinduism

As he grew older, his jealousy grew with him. Everybody would be around the cradle looking at the baby, and Ramu would put up a tremendous act of falling down. There was nothing he did not do to garner the attention that he thought was rightfully his! Soon, the jealousy had turned into hatred.

Vidhya, who did not understand any of this, cried over his behaviour till her eyes turned red. Her dearest Ramanna did not at all like her, she would tell Radhamma. "He loves you. He does not know that yet.", she would tell her daughter.

RAMU

Like every other morning, that day, Ramu rolled around in his bed for an hour before he finally got up; and the day's routine followed. He picked up a neem twig from a bunch of twigs lying on the slab, not bothering to distinguish his twig from others'. He didn't understand the fuss around it. A twig is a twig, he would tell himself. Lazily brushing his teeth, he wondered yet again of the ghost he had *almost* seen last night. If only his sister too had heard the plate crashing.

Having woken up, he had tried to get her to act as evidence for whatever transpired in the night. But no matter how many times he asked her, she simply scratched her head confusedly. A frustrated Ramu walked over to the bathing area and sat down to wait for Amma.

Soon, Radhamma had Ramu and Vidhya ready and fed. All her morning household chores done, she set out for the nearby forest to fetch firewood. Radhamma called out to their immediate neighbour Kamali, and told her to keep an eye on the children and their house while she was gone.

Ramu often wondered why she bothered telling the old lady next-door to take care of the house at all. He had never seen her keeping an eye on the house. Not even once. But moments before Radhamma got back, the cunning Kamali would walk to their house and sit by the door, as if waiting for her. No matter how many times Ramu told her how the old woman tricked her, Radhamma paid no heed. She never put him in charge of the house.

And worse, she did not trust him with Vidhya. So, she tied him to a pole that they tied the cattle to when they bathed them. And his sister sat on the door-step talking to him. There was no way he could run away from that! There he would remain, till Radhamma came back an hour later, with a stack of wood on her head.

Initially, the neighbours had all opposed when Radhamma tied little Ramu thus. But as days went by, having been on the receiving end of his mischief one too many times, they agreed with Radhamma's precautionary measures. It was only for an hour, after all, they encouraged her.

Now, with Radhamma out of sight, he began humming the song he had heard in his father's precious transistor the previous night. As much as he hated being tied, Ramu liked discovering new things to do without his hands. He tried drawing a full circle around the pole with his bare feet. When he was about to make the ends of his shabbily drawn circle meet, his friend from the neighbouring cluster came running over to him.

"Aye Ramu, that wicked ghost Ramachari is nearby now, hiding in a haystack. Manja and his friends have all surrounded the haystack to make sure Ramachari doesn't slip away this time too. Quick, let me untie you. We have to catch him today; otherwise, he will keep attacking us all!", the boy who was called Pani, spoke with great urgency.

"But Anna should not go anywhere till Radhamma comes!", Vidhya whispered.

Paying no heed to her words, the two ran towards the haystack Pani mentioned, hand in hand. No shouts from Vidhya could stop them.

While they ran, Ramu could not help but feel sad. He was disappointed with Ramachari for having been caught.

For a year now, it was Ramachari who had kept them engaged. The boys who were still young for school, but old enough to feel easily bored, had spent all their time plotting ways to catch Ramachari. It had all begun with the story that one of the boys had heard, when he went to buy a coconut from Puttajji's Angadi*:

Ramachari, one of the leaders of the village, was an evil man. He was tall and lean, and had a long moustache, the ends of which were said to touch his ears. The entire village shuddered at the sight of him. Doors and windows were shut, as he walked by the houses. Because, with him was an ever-hungry dog that he let loose if anybody displeased him. There had been many instances when poor men, who were not leaders, had asked Ramachari why he had to be the leader and not them. An angry man then, Ramachari had let his lean white dog answer their questions. The men never spoke again, because they had all died. Thus, Ramachari had turned out to be a threat to the peaceful little village. Everyone in Ganehalli lived in great misery. Those were the days when transistors played only tragic songs. The village was gloomy. But one day, tired of his antics, the boys' fathers had decided to vanquish him. Coming up with a plan in no time, they assembled at night by the only well from which Ramachari's dog drank water at all. Fortunately, when Ramachari reached the well that night, he was alone! The men surrounded him, tied his limbs and threw him into the well, thereby saving the village. But that night, Ramachari's ghost had hovered above them, promising to avenge his death by taking the life of every man in Ganehalli. It was up to the

* A shop

boys to find and kill the ghost of Ramachari, if at all it was possible to kill ghosts.

From the day they heard the story, or claimed to have heard it, every little boy was thrilled. There were doubts and questions that nobody ever dared to voice out. If one asked, 'Where's Ramachari's dog then?', the rest of them would mock him and cautiously ignore the question. Nobody knew what had happened to the lean white dog. Why, nobody really knew who it was that went to buy a coconut at all! In fact, when Ramu had run over to Puttajji's to verify the facts with her, she had simply told him she did not sell coconuts, ever. But Ramu did not breathe a word about it. They had a mission in hand. He was not prepared to ruin the chances of him becoming the saviour of their village.

From that day, the boys each narrated their many encounters with the wicked Ramachari's ghost. In every story, Ramachari was guilty of a heinous crime like eating away the Golis* they played with, for one; and the boy narrating the story, a hero who whacked the marbles out of the troublesome ghost's belly. Soon, Ramachari was all that the boys could think about. They became more creative as days passed, and were desperate to come up with the bravest story that the other children approved of and *envied.* They had all, together, attempted to kill the ghost multiple times. They had thrown pails of water from the well he drowned in, on a pole Ramachari

---

* Marbles

was said to be sitting on. They had wrapped a Dhoti* around a tree Ramachari was said to be sleeping in, and thrashed it with sticks and branches lying around. But in no story did Ramachari's ghost ever die. Because, there was an unsaid rule that Ramachari cannot be vanquished. Because if he was, the boys too would perish of boredom.

By the time Pani and Ramu reached the site, the rest of the boys from their group had already gathered. That was one thing about their group – never did they leave out anybody during their missions, no matter what. Even if Ramachari was sitting on one's neck and threatening to break it, the boys would drag the story's climax with numerous valorous twists, to accommodate every boy's presence.

When Ramu and Pani showed up, the boys told them how, in the meanwhile, Ramachari had tried to escape; and how they had chased him back to the haystack by pelting stones.

With their dramatic recounting done, they got down to business.

"He is hiding in the haystack! If we burn it right away, he will be gone for good!", one boy said.

* A garment worn by males, tied around the waist and extending to cover their legs

There was rush and excitement, and they could barely stand still. Soon, a debate broke out as to who would light the fire. They had come prepared. There was a matchbox waiting for the rightful warrior.

While every boy stated, very noisily, that he would be the one to light the fire, no one really wanted to. They prayed in secret, to not be the chosen one. Their stories were getting bigger, and scarier. They wanted it to stop. They wanted to go back home. But nobody dared say it out loud, lest they are mocked by the group and cast aside.

After a while, the boys decided it would be Ramu who would save the village from its misery. The youngest in his group, Ramu was torn between the fear of fire, and the pride of being the chosen one. A little doubtful, he stood quietly looking at the boys.

"Come on, Ramu! Let's finish off this Ramachari. We have had enough of him!", the boys called out, with great gusto. Everyone wanted him to be the saviour. At first gingerly, little Ramu got carried away by all the things his friends said.

The eldest boy, who was eight years old, picked up the matchbox and handed it to Ramu. When he held it, a strange sense of fear crept into his heart. It had nothing to do with Ramachari. It was to do with himself. He had never lit a matchstick in his life. Why, Radhamma hadn't ever let him *touch* one. How was he to tell it to the boys who looked at him with eager eyes? He felt ashamed, and tears welled up in his eyes.

He turned away from them to face the haystack and blinked hard as he fumbled with the matchbox. Slowly, he popped the box open. Taking out a matchstick, he tried recollecting how Radhamma always lit the kerosene stove at home. She would scratch the brown tip of the stick against the cheetah-like rough patches on the box. He carefully mimicked her actions from his memory. After only two attempts, he saw a spark of fire at the tip of the stick. Before anyone could realize, Ramu had thrown the lit stick into the haystack, afraid he would burn his fingers.

A huge fire-giant hovered over the children, as it greedily devoured all of the village's haystacks that had been lined up for the cattle, in only moments. Terrified, the boys ran a safe distance away and saw the fire burn on.

'It was supposed to burn only that one stack Ramachari was sleeping in', they all thought, shivering. What if the whole village burned away this way? Crying, the boys screamed for the villagers to come and stop the deadly fire. Luckily for them, after tremendous efforts, the fire died! The village was saved.

RAMU AND RADHAMMA

Closing the door behind her, Radhamma walked into the house with Ramu in her arms. He had not been able to even walk.

When she found him, he was standing with a tear-streaked face, his lips quivering and his body shivering. Hurriedly picking her child up, Radhamma had pushed past the crowd that had gathered there. By then, all of the village knew it was Ramu who had lit the haystacks, with words of encouragement from some of their own children. Not a word was uttered. Not with Radhamma looking like a starving Tigress waiting to pounce on anyone who dared to point their fingers towards her son. Hugging him close to her chest, she rushed home. He wouldn't have done whatever he did without anybody telling him to, she told herself. While he was mischievous, Ramu was a naive boy.

After having fed him, she put him to sleep. He was scared stiff, the poor boy. When he woke up, she quietly bathed him, scrubbing away small patches of soot on his skin. Then she gave him a glass of paanaka which he quickly gulped down.

"Go out!", he snapped at Vidhya who had not left his side ever since he came back home. She quietly walked out and sat by the doorstep.

Ramu slowly looked up to see Radhamma's face. His eyes welled up again, and words rushed out of his mouth. He narrated everything that had happened all through the year. Right from the first time they had decided to save the village from Ramachari's ghost. Weeping, he told her it was a secret that no adults knew. Radhamma was appalled. So much had happened under her very nose, and she had not had the slightest idea. Mentally reprimanding herself for having allowed this to last so long, she waited for him to tell every last bit of the story that he was dying to tell. His teary eyes gleamed with pride when he told her how he had, recollecting her actions, lit the matchstick.

After having heard everything that he had to say, Radhamma could not help but laugh at her silly child. Hugging him, she told him how he could have burned the whole village, and worse, himself. She shuddered at the thought.

Wiping away his tears, she massaged his feet and palms as she spoke.

"Ghosts are not evil, Ramu. Let me tell you what your Ajji told me when I was your age. I used to be very scared of the dark, because that's when the ghosts come out, don't they? Ajji told me then, that ghosts are not very unlike us. The only difference between us and them is that we have a form, and they don't; that we're alive, and they are not. Like you, I grew up listening to stories of ghosts wandering in our village. Not everybody saw them, so not everybody believed them. But all who saw them, understood one thing: the ghosts in our Ganehalli are pitifully harmless.

Everyone who dies, goes to the sky to live among the stars above. Like Ajji and Thatha. But there are those who die with a strong desire in their heart, that never came true while they lived. Those are the ones that roam around in our village as ghosts. They show themselves to those they believe can understand their plight, and help them go to the stars. If anything, ghosts are poor creatures! How can you be afraid of them?".

All through this speech, Ramu had barely breathed. He liked what his mother was telling him. If that's what ghosts are about, then he had no need to worry!

"Then, what about Ramachari? Did he too have a wish that never came true?" he asked, now feeling sorry for poor Ramachari.

Laughing, Radhamma shook her head.

"Who? Our dear old Ramachari? He was the oldest man in our village, when he passed away a few years ago. The whole village loved him, and his house was always packed with people who went to visit him. Till days before he passed away on his 109th birthday, the villagers stacked the table next to his bed with fruits of all kinds. He was a kind man, our dear old Ramachari. Always smiling, and always telling everyone stories – like the one you told me. I would not be surprised if it had been Ramachari himself, who came up with this story. Even after his death, the jolly old man has kept you boys entertained! But burning the village down is another matter! Promise me you won't ever do anything foolish."

Happy that it was all over, Ramu promised her he would behave, and behave he did; so well, that Radhamma did not find the need to tie him up anymore. Little Ramu was growing up.

Weeks passed, and Ramu helped his mother in any way he could. With the task of catching Ramachari out of their hands, the boys lead a dull life. So dull, that helping with chores seemed exciting.

Even then, he would not play with Vidhya.

It was one weekend that Ramu outdid himself. He helped clean the house and bring small pails of water for Radhamma to bathe the cattle with. He did this and that. He worked so hard that he slept very early that night.

When he woke up the next morning, Radhamma gave him a whopping 5 Rs. coin. He looked at it, and then at her, and at the coin again; as if she would take it from him anytime. Seconds later, when she still had not snatched it away, he shrieked in joy. It was for him!

He knew what to do with it. He would stop by Puttajji's Anngadi and buy the big ball of chocolate Pani simply would not stop talking about. He would eat it all up. Then, he would walk to Pani's house to tell him that he too had eaten the chocolate ball; and that Puttajji had told him his was the biggest ever.

Jumping out of his bed, he brushed his teeth and bathed himself hurriedly, without waiting for Radhamma. The coin safe in his pocket, Ramu rushed to the door. The wait had been torturous and he couldn't take it any longer.

He ran past the houses in his cluster, and then a long stretch of land that had once held numerous haystacks.

Ramu winced, but he kept running. Panting for breath, he finally arrived at the shop - the dream destination for all the children in his village. Puttajji stood inside, smiling her toothy smile.

"I am here for the big chocolate ball!", Ramu exclaimed shakily, unable to contain his excitement. Oh, how long had he waited for it!

Grinning, Puttajji placed a chocolate ball into Ramu's little hands. Walking a few metres away from the shop, he stopped under a huge tree. He pulled out his father's kerchief from his pocket, spread it on the ground below the tree, and sat down to relish the chocolate. It was wrapped in blue foil. Peeling it off without the chocolate sticking to it required skill.

As he began peeling, he heard someone sighing. He turned to his left, there was nothing. Nor was there anything to his right.

He returned to his task of removing the wrapper. He heard another meek sigh. When he looked up this time, he saw a whiff of smoke.

Before long, the smoke cleared and he saw the ghost of a boy. The frail little boy stood leaning against the tree. His breath caught in his throat, Ramu stared at the boy with his eyes ready to pop out. A thousand questions whirled in his head, and he was able to catch hold of none. It was a ghost! He had met a ghost when he least expected to. He was so shocked; it did not occur to him to get scared.

Besides, Radhamma had told him that ghosts only showed themselves to those who would understand them. He was still debating what to say to the little ghost of a boy, when he spoke up.

"Why did you not get the spinning top?" he asked, in a high-pitched squeaky voice, seeming really disappointed with Ramu.

"What? Why?", Ramu was confused.

"Why did you not get the Buguli with white and blue lines?".

The ghost must have been 5, Ramu thought. His lisp had still not left him. How stupid! Just like his sister! Ramu had lost his lisp very early, he had often heard his mother tell the neighbouring women.

"Bugurrri, you mean?", he said, to emphasize clearly the fact that he did not have a lisp. "My brother has a Buguri*. I can play with it whenever I want. So, I don't need another one." he defended himself.

"Youl blothel plays with you?", the boy asked him in awe, his eyes wide. "Is he also big, like you?"

"No, he is bigger. I have two brothers. Both are very big, but they lend me their Buguri to play with, if I want; or we all play together!", Ramu explained sincerely, although he was confused with the interrogation.

"You all play togethel…", the boy mumbled, his eyes sad.

"I don't understand. Why do you want the Buguri?" Ramu asked him.

* A spinning wooden top

It was the eve of his birthday. Rishi sat on the cement slab by his house and watched his brothers playing a Buguri match. Like every other day, they had refused when he had asked if he too could play. He did not have a Buguri. If only he had had one, they would have let him play with them. Few years older, they seldom spoke to Rishi. But when the family sat down for dinner together, they would pat his head, ruffle his hair, and acknowledge him. That was the part of the day he most loved; not when his mother gave him an extra piece of jaggery, or when his father took him around on his bicycle. It was his brothers' pats that made him the happiest. Oh, how he wished he could grow up soon and play with them. For that, all he needed was a Buguri!

When he turned 4, he had wanted to ask his mother for a Buguri. But that was a time when the floods had struck Ganehalli, and their livelihood was at stake. There was no food at home. Amma and Appa spent most of their days fighting. Rishi hated the floods, because they made Amma cry. He dared not make his demands at a time like that. Instead, he quietly went about helping her, taking up extra chores on himself. But the fights only grew bigger. Sometimes, Appa would throw things at Amma. While his brothers stayed out of the fights, Rishi would run and stand in front of his mother as if to shield her, with folded hands and a tear-streaked face. That was the only thing that could stop Appa – Rishi's face. He was the apple of their eye, after all; the child they doted on.

Once a happy family, poverty had pushed them into a dark world where there was nothing but accusations, fights, and tears.

"You are turning 5 tomorrow. What do you want?", his mother's voice woke him from his daydream.

He could not ask her for a top. Amma did not have the money, he knew. He was still gazing at his brothers when his mother spoke again.

"Okay. I know what you want. Be a good boy, and wake up early tomorrow. You can go get your Buguri!", she laughed and pushed a coin into his pocket.

Rishi jumped out of her lap and looked at her in disbelief. He could not believe his luck. Tugging at her saree, he sang a song so off-tune, his mother laughed.

"Nanna Buguli…nanna Buguli…nanna Buguli".

"I am not sending you to the shop till you can say it right. Buu…gu... rrri. Say it?", she laughed.

"Bu..Buguli…Bugu…lliiii!" Rishi giggled, as she tickled him.

This was going to be his best birthday.

Early next morning, Rishi was the first to wake up. He was brimming with excitement. Taking the coin from under his pillow, he rehearsed how he would buy the Buguri from Puttajji. He would ask her for the white one with blue lines. Holding his hand forward, he pretended to wrap his hand around the Buguri, and said 'Thank you'.

Soon, Rishi was all clad in a yellow shirt, handed down by his second brother. It had been kept for special occasions. His oiled hair was neatly combed to the side, and a streak of Kumkuma* on his forehead swore to protect him from all the evils. He went to his parents to seek blessings.

"Live long, you sweet child!", they said in unison.

His brothers laughed at him and ruffled his hair. He giggled excitedly, and walked towards the door. He was finally going to get the Buguri! He would finally be able to play with his brothers.

Squealing, he ran down the street, when he heard a plate crash. Was it from his house? Clutching the coin tightly, Rishi froze in his tracks. When he heard another crash, he ran back to his house. He saw his brothers sitting on the slab outside, like they always did when there was a fight. He ran faster, and got home in time to see his father throwing a glass of Shaavige Payasa** Amma had made for his birthday. It fell down with a crash, followed by Amma's wails and abuses. He shut the door behind him and stood looking at his parents. He did not understand what they were talking about; it had only been a few minutes since he stepped out. But he knew something very wrong had happened. Appa looked so angry; Rishi was scared.

Hurling a string of abuses at Amma, Appa picked the iron table that stood in the corner, causing the contents on it to fall down. Lifting it over his head, he aimed it

---

* Vermilion powder donned during auspicious occasions/after prayers in Hinduism

** Vermicelli Pudding

at her. Was he really going to throw it at her? Rishi ran to stand in-front of her, his hands folded, his face tear-streaked, while his precious coin lay buried in the mud in-front of his house. He hadn't even realized.

"Rishi, you go get your Buguri!", his mother smiled at him through her tears, gently pushing him to the door. He did not budge.

Struggling to keep her smile on for little Rishi's sake, she pushed him towards the door again. Stronger. At the same time, Appa shifted his aim from Amma and threw the table at the door, with all the strength he could muster. He had to vent his anger. He couldn't go on after seeing Rishi standing with a tear-streaked face on his very birthday.

Alas, nobody expected the events to coincide! A confused Rishi who was pushed to the door, froze when he saw the table flying towards him. He heard his parents scream just as the table crushed him to the door. The rusted sharp edges cut through his throat. This is why Amma never let him go near that table. The door flew open, and Rishi tumbled down the stairs like a Buguri himself.

His family went rushing to him, screaming in agony. But little could they save Rishi.

He rolled his eyes above looking for his coin. Further down the path he lay on, lay his precious little coin. It was a muddy mess.

"Nanna Buguli?", he said helplessly, as tears streamed down his face.

In a blood-soaked yellow shirt, with Kumkuma smeared across his forehead and sand sticking to his oily hair, little Rishi reluctantly shut his eyes forever. He wouldn't ever get hold of a Buguri, would he?

"You should have bought the white Buguli", Rishi snapped, when his story came to an end.

Ramu did not say a word. He looked at the ball of chocolate and then at Rishi. Then, he got up and walked straight to Puttajji's store. Scanning through the toys that hung above him, Ramu's eyes landed on a bunch of Tops. They lit up when he found the Buguri with white and blue lines. Struggling for words, he asked Puttajji to exchange his chocolate ball for the Buguri. When she refused, his eyes welled up. A confused Puttajji hurriedly took the chocolate ball from him, and offered him the white and blue Buguri. Ramu thanked her with folded hands.

Running back to the tree, he held the Buguri in front of Rishi's ghost for him to get a good look at it. Seeing his pleased face, Ramu spun the top on the ground multiple times, before handing it over to Rishi.

"Nanna Buguli…*" he smiled as he closed his fingers around the top.

Spinning, it fell onto the ground and the whiff of smoke disappeared forever.

---

* My spinning wooden top

Ramu stood transfixed, attempting to understand whatever had happened. The Buguri lay beneath his feet. The noise of the crashing plate from a few weeks ago might not have been real; but this was as real as it could get.

Rishi must have gone to the stars, he thought. He decided he would look for the little boy among the stars that night. Ramu too had finally met a ghost. Nobody would believe him. Why, he himself could not believe it.

He picked up the Buguri with great care; like it was holy. Then, he ran back home.

"Where's Vidhya?", he asked Radhamma, gasping for breath. Before she could answer, he rushed inside. Vidhya was sleeping.

"What a useless being! Who sleeps at a time like this?", he muttered to himself as he sat down by her side.

Minutes later, when she did not wake up, Ramu coughed loudly. She barely stirred in her sleep.

Unable to wait any longer, he tapped her on the shoulder.

"Get up! Why are you sleeping? Let us play!", he snapped.

That was enough for Vidhya's sleep to disappear. Without a word, she sat up and looked at him with her eyes ready to pop out.

"Here, hold this. I brought this for you. You are very small! But, it's okay, I will teach you how to play with it!", he said in one breath.

Before Vidhya could nod, he spoke again, "I will play with you only if you promise me not to become a ghost."

A confused Vidhya placed the palm of her right hand on her head, and pinched her neck with her left hand.

"Promise.", she said, in all sincerity.

That evening the house echoed with the siblings' squeaky giggles.

Author Bio

Yashaswini Balasubramanyam hails from the bustling city of Chennai. Having always been surrounded by a rich tapestry of narratives, she has been a lover of stories since she was young. She believes that life is a never-ending source of inspiration and that there are countless stories waiting to be told.

> "One only needs to look around to watch the world turn into a canvas brimming with vibrant stories.", she says.

This first book represents the fruition of a lifelong dream and the beginning of a journey that she hopes will touch the hearts of her readers. In her stories, she blends reality with the surreal, inviting readers to take a journey into a world of endless possibilities. She is working on her next book and is eager to share her perspective with the world again.

Acknowledgments

I am grateful to RV, my #1, for snapping at me every time I said I was apprehensive of publishing. For pushing me to take a break just to write. He has quietly gone about removing every little obstacle there has been in my way, and made room for me to do what I most love doing – writing stories. Without him, I wouldn't be (almost) fearlessly chasing my dreams. The journey that saw me writing tales and poems for him…because of him…has taken exciting turns through time!

To Arunima Aunty, for 1. Her helpful feedback on every story in this book. 2. The 3-hour-long guidance call. 3. For a much-needed, awesomely-timed boost! Thanks again, Aunty!

To Vallish who ranks second in the "Who has read these stories the maximum number of times?" list. The first being me, of course. He has patiently read them from when they were chaotic synopses to when they were baby drafts, to when they became full-fledged stories; besides urging me to "just go publish a book already"! Thanks for the helpful feedback and support, Sensei of Awesomeness!

To Jeni, who has been reading my stories from back when I scribbled them onto loose sheets during our school days. My first audience. She read through handwritten words that were struck; words that I had invented because

I could; and worst of all, words written in the infamous SMS language. She gave reviews that were, all of them, BIASED! My biggest motivator!

To Roomana, who is as excited about this book as Agnes was about the fluffy Unicorn. She has been with me on this journey since my Wattpad 'chick lit writing' days back when I was in college (All traces of those stories have been safely disposed of). She was both a ruthless reviewer and a supportive cheerleader when I was writing this book.

Lastly, but most importantly, to my family! No project of mine, big or small, has gone by without deafening cheers from my big family! To all the lovely people who have always urged me on in this journey: You know who you are!

www.ingramcontent.com/pod-product-compliance
Lightning Source LLC
La Vergne TN
LVHW041159150826
845673LV00001B/216

* 9 7 9 8 8 8 9 3 5 9 6 5 4 *